W9-CMQ-460

ARTHUR SLADE

HarperCollins*PublishersLtd*

Published by HarperCollins Publishers Ltd.

First edition

HarperCollins books may be purchased for educational, business, or sales promotional use through our Special Markets Department.

HarperCollins Publishers Ltd
2 Bloor Street East, 20th Floor
Toronto, Ontario, Canada
M4W 1A8

www.harpercollins.ca

Library and Archives Canada Cataloguing in Publication

Slade, Arthur G. (Arthur Gregory)
   The hunchback assignments / Arthur Slade.

ISBN 978-1-55468-354-3

I. Title.

PS8587.L343H85 2009   JC813'.54   C2009-902368-7

Printed and bound in the United States
HC 9 8 7 6 5 4 3 2 1

For Tori,
with all my love

The Foxhound

Six hunting hounds had perished in previous experiments. Dr. Cornelius Hyde crouched in the cellar of his manor staring over his spectacles at Magnus, the last surviving hound. The iron cage was sturdy, its door locked tight, and the dog looked healthy except for his drooping head. He had survived the operation that replaced his skull, jaws and teeth with metal, but the weight of it all was too much for him to bear for long periods of time. He needed strength and ferocity. Soon, Hyde hoped, these needs would be dealt with.

Hyde opened a hatch at the top of the cage and carefully attached a coiled wire to each of the bolts that extended out of the hound's shoulders. The dog didn't move. The doctor then connected the wire to a gyroscope sitting nearby on a broken chair.

Hyde sat in another chair at a table. His smooth, ink-stained hands trembled as he jotted down: *March 7, 1860, 7:35 p.m. Trial 7.* He felt certain that this time the elixir would have the desired effect. He hadn't slept or washed in days, having spent every hour measuring the elements precisely, mixing them and boiling the compound in a glass beaker. He didn't wish to see his favourite foxhound suffer with the same tremors and terrors that had consumed the other hounds as they succumbed to a slow, contorted death.

Hyde spoke hoarsely. "You are a good companion." Magnus raised his head with some effort and wagged his tail. His master winced and ran a hand through his greying shock of hair. It had been months since he'd had it cut. "This is for science," he explained tenderly. "Science. Mother Nature's design has failed you, but mine will not."

Magnus went on wagging. He was nine years old. His back was lean and well muscled, his front legs as straight as posts. The dog had always been loyal and even-tempered; not once had he snapped in anger. He had hunted alongside Hyde in the days when the doctor needed to feign interest in such folly in order to procure funding from lords and gentlemen. Their contributions had enabled him to continue his research. Those days were long past.

The members of the Society of Science in London now treated him with scorn, accusing him of madness and tampering with the natural order, as though changing a creature's chemistry and structure for the better was something beyond evil. Scientific heresy! they'd shouted. They cut off his funds. Half the scientists were members of Parliament. They convinced the government to declare his experiments a crime.

A crime! The more he thought of those fat, arrogant politicians debating the value of his work, the more he became enraged. He pictured them voting to outlaw his experiments, the Society of Science dullards nodding their heads.

"Fools," he whispered. "Stupid, mindless fools."

A few days after the vote, constables kicked open the door to his city home and confiscated most of his equipment. He fled to his country manor to conduct his experiments in the cellar. He scrounged for funds, and was reduced to using the last of his inheritance and his remaining few beakers and compounds to carry out trials upon his own animals. Soon he would be dragged away to debtor's prison.

Above him the floorboards creaked. He listened intently, ears buzzing. Until recently he would have assumed it to be his manservant, but Dr. Hyde had dismissed him a fortnight earlier. Could it be a constable? He waited for a full minute, finally deciding the sound was only the shifting of the house. It grumbled every time the weather changed.

Hyde picked up a flask of blood-red liquid from the table, the burnt-almond smell making him cringe. He'd been working on this tincture now for seven years. "For the sake of knowledge," he said to the air.

He carefully filled the bowl in the cage. The hound stared at his master, his neck even weaker from the weight of his metal head, his tail limp.

"Go on, Magnus," Hyde urged, his heart near breaking. "Drink. Drink your medicine."

But the dog wouldn't move, and Hyde couldn't help but wonder if Magnus knew he was in danger. Over the last few weeks his keen ears surely had picked up the agitated barks, unearthly howls and final whimpers of his brethren. Did he understand that he would be next? For a long time the dog watched Hyde, though he could barely hold his head up. He began lapping at the tincture, his pink tongue rubbing on metal teeth. He kept his eyes on Hyde. The doctor swallowed hard, bile in his throat.

Beside him on the table was a clockwork model of a hound, about one-sixteenth life-size. He patted it and gears clicked and spun. The metallic dog moved its head from side to side. Dr. Hyde smiled; imagine what he might create if only he could get his hands on the proper resources!

He reached for his quill and notebook. The dog grimaced and revealed silver teeth. His head was higher now. For the first time ever Hyde heard the sweet-natured dog growl. Magnus's head jerked from side to side, as though he didn't recognize his surroundings. His attention settled on the cage's hinges and locks, and he attacked them again and again. Sparks flew, metal bent and Hyde stepped back. He crouched, ready to run, but the cage was holding together.

Under the gas light, the doctor wrote copious notes, dipping his quill frantically into the inkwell. He was so absorbed in recording his observations that he didn't hear the cellar door open. He didn't see a figure steal down the stairway and slip into the shadows.

Magnus howled, arching his back until it pressed against the top of the cage. He banged his head against the side, making the bars bend. If his skull had been made of bone it would have shattered. Hyde's eyes grew wide. The hound seemed to have grown larger, his muscles swelling, quivering under his thin hide. His paws were bigger, his nails more like claws, and they dug into the iron-plated floor.

The beast threw himself at the door of the cage and the whole contraption inched closer to the doctor, who continued to scribble down each change in behaviour. Magnus stopped to glare at Hyde hungrily, and attacked the cage again.

Hyde was amazed at the dog's increased stamina. No sign of weariness. No drooping neck. Then, when his fury was at its highest, the gyroscope slowly began to turn. Hyde held his breath as the machine spun so quickly it blurred, the base vibrating. It fell to the floor and thumped around until it disconnected from the wires, and stopped. His theory was true! Some inner power that could be harnessed existed. The tincture had brought it out of the dog.

It was half an hour before Magnus let out a yelp, whimpered, and finally deflated. He looked affectionately at Hyde as if to apologize for his outburst. Hyde moved over to the cage, still making notes. The hound's chest heaved. Hyde felt a smile cross his face. Alive! Magnus had survived the tincture's effects. The next task would be to find a way to control the hound once it had been enhanced. What a wonder he would be then. The perfect hound. Ready to hunt much larger game than ducks.

Hounds would be only the beginning. The true test would be to discover the tincture's effect on a man.

A soft clapping shocked him out of his imaginings.

"*Bravissimo*, Doctor." It was the voice of a woman with an unusual accent.

Hyde jerked around so fast he nearly toppled over. The intruder was on the far side of the cellar, cloaked in darkness.

"How did you get in?"

"Through the door, of course. It is a shame that someone of your stature is in such severe financial straits that you had to dismiss your staff."

"Who are you?"

"I am the servant of a great cause. Our organization has had its eyes on you for years now, Dr. Hyde."

He pointed his quill in the direction of her voice. "I'm doing nothing wrong. Are you with the inspectors?"

She laughed coldly. "No. I do not represent lackeys of your government. As I said, I am the humble servant of a guild of like-minded people—people who are unafraid to challenge the status quo. Let us just say my employer is very interested in your research. You have a marvellous mind, to understand clockwork and chemistry so well. We desire both, especially your potion."

"It's a drug. Not a potion."

She moved into the light and Hyde sucked in his breath. She was lithe and pale and beautiful, her bright red hair tied in complicated braids. Hyde had long believed himself immune to such beauty, but he couldn't stop looking at her, couldn't think of a word to say. Then he noticed her left hand was a hook, the metal glinting in the low light. He adjusted his spectacles, squinting.

"Your hand," he said. "I would have replaced it with a much better instrument."

"Oh, I believe you," she said, hiding the hook behind

her back. "But after all, it was just a hand. A man with your vision deserves a much larger canvas. You would like that, wouldn't you, Dr. Hyde?"

He glanced at the sleeping form of Magnus, at the clockwork model on the table, at the crumbling walls of the cellar, then back at the woman. "Yes. Yes, I would."

"Then, Doctor, we have so very much to discuss."

CHAPTER 1

Abomination

The large carriage rattled with grotesqueries—bones of cats and pigs strung up as wind chimes, bleached bear skulls dangling from wires, and three shrunken monkey heads mounted on posts. Their glass eyes stared out at the approaching winter. Bells that hung from reins tinkled, warning away wandering spirits. Four horses pulled the carriage, hip bones protruding from their bedraggled flesh, hides scarred by thousands of whippings. Huddled behind them in a thick, worn coat and muffler was a grizzled old man.

The tall, slim gentleman watched the carriage approach down a rutted, moonlit road. A cold breath of wind tested his knee-length greatcoat, but he didn't shiver. His close-cropped hair, white since birth, glowed in the dull light. His sharp eyes scanned the carriage, from the shivering driver to the clicking bones, and finally rested on the words MERVEILLES ET MORTE, written in red across the carriage's side. They appeared and disappeared with the swinging of a lantern.

Merveilles et Morte. Wonders and Death. He hoped that a wonder waited inside. He had spent his life and a good part of his fortune seeking out those with special talents. The reports about this particular sideshow travelling through Provence were extremely promising.

At one side of the carriage a flag snapped in the wind, its skull-and-crossbones flashing. Pirates? An almost imperceptible smile crossed the gentleman's lips. These weren't pirates. Charlatans and gypsy-souls, yes. But pirates? No. He had met real pirates on the open seas; had summarily put them to death.

The gentleman held up his hand and the driver pulled on the reins. The horses slowed to a stop and snorted out frosty air, stomping their hooves.

"I would like to see your display," the gentleman said. His French was perfect, his accent Parisian.

"Oh, yes, yes, *monsieur*! I will be only too happy to show you." The old man set his whip into its holder and climbed down, babbling excitedly. "It is a marvellous collection! The greatest this side of the Nile. Balms to cure cholera. Elixirs to stave off death itself. I have a fine ruby necklace, straight from Cleopatra's tomb, that will make any arthritic condition vanish. And it will soften the skin, strengthen the bones—"

"I'm not interested in trinkets or balms," the gentleman cut in. "I want to see your prize attraction."

A door behind the bench slid open and a hag stuck her head out. Her eyes gleamed within a nest of wrinkles. She was a hundred years old if she was a day. "It is an expensive view," she rasped. "An extremely rare specimen."

The gentleman opened a gloved hand. Two golden coins caught the moonlight. "I assume this will cover it."

The hag nodded and waved a hand at the driver.

"Yes. Yes, *monsieur*," the driver said, palming the coins. "Of course. Come right this way."

He led the gentleman to the rear door of the carriage. More bones were strung across the back, charms against death. The gentleman grinned. Only savages relied on such charms and magic to defeat the unknown. Learned men relied on logic.

The old man took a key from his pocket and unlocked the door with a brassy click. He swung it open and warm moist air belched out. The gentleman didn't turn his nose from the rotten smell. He had encountered much worse on the Crimean battlefields.

"Inside, that is where the prizes are!" The driver tried to climb in, but the gentleman placed a hand on his shoulder and pulled him out of the way.

"I will enter alone."

"But, *monsieur*, only I can explain the origins. The magic! The mystery! The restorative power of each item."

"I don't need explanations."

The driver nodded, and the gentleman stepped up into the fetid compartment, stooping to keep from banging his head. The cramped space was poorly lit by one lantern swinging on a wire. In a moment his eyes had adjusted and the details became clear. There were Canopic jars, glass bottles with hairless, pink creatures, tiny coffins marked with hieroglyphics, shrunken heads dangling from wires and the stuffed body of a half-cat, half-rabbit. He had seen such stuffed creatures before, but this was a very good represen-tation—it didn't even look as though it had been stitched together. He moved through the collection quickly, ducking under the lantern and squeezing between a stuffed snake and a giant bat with marbles for eyes.

At the far end of the carriage was a cage draped in black cloth. He leaned in close. From behind the fabric he heard something wheezing. Without hesitation he pulled away the cover.

Two eyes, one larger than the other, goggled up at him in fright. Above them was a tinge of red hair set on a rough-hewn, pockmarked skull. The gentleman flinched; he had been expecting something ugly, but this was beyond his imagining. A true wretch of a creature crouched in the cage, pressing against the bars. It wore a jackal-fur vest, which was ill-fitting due to the enormous hump on its back. Pity wormed its way into the gentleman's heart.

The unfortunate monster couldn't be more than a year old. It was standing upright, but the small cage forced it to bend its neck, emphasizing its hump. On the bottom of the cage a plaque read, L'ENFANT DU MONSTRE.

The gentleman could not stop staring. The specimen's arms looked strong, and its legs were unnaturally muscled but bowed and crooked. Nature had been particularly cruel.

The thing was shivering, but seemed to grow curious. It blinked, mewling softly. The gentleman peered at it impas-sively. This had been a wasted journey; three days' travel from London to Provence only to find a child imprisoned by its ugliness. His informant had spoken so highly of this prize, had said the creature was beyond description and value. Ah! That scoundrel would feel the lash of his anger. The gentleman had lost time, when he had none to lose. All the while England's enemies would be inching closer to their goals.

He turned away, but the creature mewled again, and whispered, "*Puh-puh-père?*"

Father? The gentleman stopped. The voice sounded so human, so mournful, and it struck a chord in the man's heart. Years ago he'd had a wife who died giving birth to their child. A boy, who had lived only long enough for his father to hold him. The gentleman swallowed. It was all in the past and best forgotten.

Yet, he turned back to the creature. By its size and shape he decided it too was a boy. A monstrous, malformed boy. The man considered whether he had any food in his pocket. Foolishness. It was time to leave.

The boy said, "*N-n-non p-p-partir,*" and gazed at him with such absolute sadness that the gentleman was transfixed. Then the boy let out a yelp, clenching his fists as though he were feeling a sharp stinging. His face contorted, becoming even uglier.

The gentleman couldn't look away. Was it possible? Was the child actually changing, his face shifting so that his features . . . softened? The boy let out a whimper. Where, moments ago, there had been a crooked nose with splayed nostrils, now the nose seemed to be straighter. It was as if, seeing the horror in the gentleman's eyes, the toddler was willing himself to change his appearance into something more attractive. The boy's brow was flatter, the eyes more even. Was it the flickering of the gaslight? The gentleman stepped closer. No, the boy's face was indeed altered. Then the child gave another yelp, like that of a wounded puppy, and shook his massive head.

The gentleman lowered the cover over the cage in amazement and took a deep breath. This monster-child was truly a wonder! Worth every moment spent away from England; worth his weight in gold. His talent could prove to be a valuable asset. His development would require years of investment, but the gentleman was good at playing the long game.

He climbed out of the carriage. The old codger was stamping his feet on the ground, hugging himself for warmth.

"I wish to buy the item," the gentleman said. "The one in the cage." He kept his voice steady, hiding his excitement.

"*Non! Non!*" The driver waved his hands. "That is not possible."

The hag limped around the corner of the carriage. "He's very precious. Very precious."

The gentleman produced a pouch of coins. "This will compensate you for your losses."

A bony arm shot out of the crone's shawl and grasped the pouch. She pried open the top and squinted inside. "*Oui* . . . that is a fair deal."

"Where did you find him?"

"He comes from far, far away," the old man said. "From

the Steppes. In the ancient land of Moldova, near the spawn-ing ground of demons and—"

"The truth," the gentleman said in a soft, threatening tone. "I demand the truth."

The hag moved a step closer. "He was abandoned near Notre Dame. We bought him from an orphanage."

The gentleman nodded. He whistled and his carriage charged out of the fog, pulled by four huge horses. Three men, clean-cut and dressed in dark greatcoats, jumped to the ground. They marched over to the gypsy carriage and, at the gentleman's command, pulled the caged monster-child from that carriage and transferred it to their own.

"Farewell," the gentleman said as he mounted the steps.

The child could be heard moaning and bumping up against the bars of his cage. There was the crack of a whip as the gentleman stepped inside, and then the elegant carriage lurched forward into the mist.

CHAPTER 2

Reflection

The boy was seated at a small wooden table. He wore black knee-length breeches, a white linen shirt and a black cravat tied carefully around his neck, every inch a young gentleman. He stared at the blank parchment for a moment and then, using a chrome-plated cedar pencil, he wrote his name with his left hand in large careful letters: *M–o–d–o*. Beside that, he wrote down the date: *October 12th, 1864*. He'd been taught how to write a year earlier, at the age of four.

No mirrors or reflective surfaces had been allowed in the room, nor in the rest of the house. The windows were boarded up and papered over; the little sunlight that fell onto his parchment entered through a skylight cupola.

Below his name he began to draw how he imagined his own face to look. Occasionally he would hold the pencil up and examine a sliver of his reflection on the smooth side of the chrome. He could make out eyes and lips, but all his features were distorted. He couldn't see his nose.

When he rubbed his face with his gnarled fingers he felt only a crooked protrusion of flesh. He kept drawing, adding a straight nose and perfectly formed ears. He chose eyes from one of his favourite illustrations of the Royals— the eyes of a prince. He'd memorized so many engravings from the books that he didn't need to open one for reference. He added a top hat, for effect. A gentleman always wore a top hat.

Through the door was a larger room with Indian clubs and dumbbells hung on one wall, and rows of wooden swords and spears hung on the opposite wall. A practice dummy, made of straw-stuffed sacks, was strung up in the middle of the room. It never failed to give Modo a shiver as it conjured the hanging he'd read about in a book. A small earth closet had been tucked into the farthest wall of the farthest room, complete with a metal wash basin.

He had spent the past four years inside the rooms of Ravenscroft. Mrs. Finchley had told him a story about how the house was named for the large number of ravens that perched on the roof and marched around the skylight. He had seen them when he climbed up the rope to press his head against the skylight to glimpse the tops of trees, his only view of the outside world. Alas, he hadn't been able to see his reflection.

The click of a distant lock made his ears prick. Someone was entering the house. He slowed the rate of his breathing, the way he'd been taught, so that his pulse wouldn't interfere with his hearing. A knife clattered in the kitchen, a drawer closed, and he heard a great sigh. It was Mrs. Finchley, no doubt feeling sad again. Modo wondered what he could do to make her happy. Perform a dance? Draw another picture?

Maybe she needed to play a game. He considered climbing up into the space above the door and clinging there to surprise her, but the last time he'd done it she'd shrieked and roundly scolded him, so he let the thought pass. A plate clattered on a countertop. She would be bringing him food. He licked his lips.

He heard another lock click; the door to the gym room squeaked open and closed, and then locked a moment later. His back was to her but he heard each step, could picture where she was. When she turned the corner into his room he said, "Mrs. Finchley, is that bread and honey for me?"

She let out a tiny huff of amazement. "You are a clever one, aren't you. But not clever enough to know that you shouldn't draw with your left hand."

"Why?"

"Because most people are right-handed and you don't want to stand out. Only the Devil draws with his left hand."

Modo shivered and switched hands; he was equally adept with his right. He continued shading the cheeks on the prince's face.

"Is this what I look like, Mrs. Finchley?" He tried to keep his voice from cracking, but failed.

She placed a plate with a piece of bread, slathered with butter and honey, in front of him. "Don't concern yourself with your appearance, Modo. You're a beautiful child in your own way."

He gazed up into her green eyes. She was gaunt and softly wrinkled. He wanted to leap up and hug her, but she had narrowed her eyes as though she had seen something disturbing.

"Why do you cringe when you look at my face?" he asked.

"Sometimes you are too observant for your own good, Modo. You remind me of my Daniel, that's all."

Modo knew her son had been killed by a runaway carriage many years before. "Was he beautiful too?"

"Yes, very. But, please, let's not speak of him."

She looked sad again, and he searched for some way to soothe her. "I nodded off reading and fell into a story."

"You really are a wonder, Modo. Reading at such a young age."

"Yes, well, it was that book you brought from—from outside—the book with the baby princess. You see, she had lost her gravity, so she floats."

"I thought you might enjoy that story. One can read only so many books about generals and military tactics."

"Oh, yes! I did enjoy it. The nurse has to hold on to her tight so she doesn't drift away. And she only laughs and never cries. In my dream I floated too, and the princess was there. But not her aunt, the witch. She wasn't in my dream, and you were the nurse."

"You have a marvellous imagination, Modo."

"Have you ever been a nurse?" he asked.

Mrs. Finchley shook her head. "No, but I once played a nurse on stage at the Theatre Royal."

"Really? Tell me more! Please!"

"That was long ago and those years are gone. I'm only a governess now."

"Oh." Modo sucked in his bottom lip for a moment, then quietly said, "Are you my mother?"

"No. I've told you many times already. I'm just here to care for you and to teach you. I don't know who your mother was."

"I see." He paused. "Wot's me teacher got for me today?"

Mrs. Finchley laughed. "That's a good Cockney accent. You began studying that only last week."

"Will we be dressing up today? I have a new character to try."

"It's Sunday, today. You know that, Modo. On Sunday you learn history. But eat first, child." Modo took two quick bites before she whispered, "Eat like a gentleman."

He ate eagerly but more slowly, at the end licking his thick lips for the last few crumbs and bits of honey. She wiped his face with a napkin. He clasped her arm firmly.

"You're still sad." She nodded, and he squeezed more tightly. "I don't want you to feel that way."

Modo looked deep into her eyes and grimaced. He felt the familiar sensation of his face shifting. As far back as he could remember, he had always been able to do this. He'd seen the locket she carried containing a miniature portrait of her son. He pictured Daniel's face.

She gasped and tried to pull her arm away, but Modo was strong for his age. His eyes grew smaller and his features compressed as though they were made of clay. His lips became thinner.

"Daniel," she whimpered. "No! No!" Tears ran down her face. With a jerk she broke Modo's grip and turned away to wipe her eyes. "No! Don't do that. Not for me."

"I only want you to be happy."

"No. It's not right. Don't."

"But it . . ." He stood a bit straighter. "It's just the way I am. You don't like it?"

"Please don't change for me. It isn't necessary."

She closed her eyes and allowed herself a few last sobs, then composed herself while Modo let his face slip back to its usual form. He blinked away tears of his own.

"Don't cry, Modo. Your eyes will be red like mine," she said. "I'm a soft, silly woman." She cupped his face and patted his shoulder, inadvertently touching his hump. "You're a sweet, beautiful boy."

Her words made him glow. He had, of course, felt his face enough that he was aware of the large protruding mole tucked next to his nose, and knew that above his right eye he had a spongy bump. Mrs. Finchley had gently called them beauty marks. But she never explained his hump in such terms. If he turned his head he could see the edge of it.

Mrs. Finchley stood and straightened her apron. "Come now, let us work on Latin history. Today, we shall read about Caesar Augustus."

"I love Suetonius," he exclaimed, following her to the bookshelves where she took down a worn copy of *De Vita Caesarum.*

Modo felt other eyes watching him, heard a soft noise. He spun around and gave a start at the sight of Tharpa, his

combat instructor, standing in the doorway, his eyes dark
and intense. Tharpa was holding a burgundy carpet bag.
Since Tharpa rarely spoke, all Modo really knew of him
was that he was from India. How had he unlocked the doors
and crept across the hardwood without so much as a creak?
Tharpa was a panther.

Modo tugged on Mrs. Finchley's elbow, and she turned
and shuddered a little when she saw Tharpa. "You're not
scheduled to train him today," she said.

Modo gave Tharpa a little wave.

Tharpa's reply was to step aside as his master strode
through the door, dressed in a fine suit. His cravat matched
his white hair. His green eyes peered intensely out of his
angular, pale face.

"Mr. Socrates!" Mrs. Finchley said. "Had I known
you were coming I certainly would have prepared tea and
biscuits."

"No need. I came on a whim. How has our pupil been?"

"He still learns so effortlessly."

Mr. Socrates crossed the room and looked down at
Modo. "It is a pleasure to see you again, Modo. Are you
obeying Mrs. Finchley in all matters?"

"Yes, Mr. Socrates."

"I see you are reading Suetonius. Good. What is your
opinion of Julius Caesar?"

"He—he was strong."

"Yes. But what was his greatest strength?"

Modo scratched at his eyebrow. "Um . . ."

"Don't preface your thoughts with 'um.' It's boorish."

"His greatest strength was that he was . . . he was . . ."
Modo searched for a word that described Caesar. *Brave?*
Intelligent? "He was very determined."

"Determination will take you a long way. Good answer,
Modo." Mr. Socrates took the carpet bag from Tharpa,
reached inside and handed Modo a book. "I think you're
ready for this. It is Colonel Graham's translation of *On War*,
by Clausewitz. The prose is clunky but passable and . . ." He
paused, picked up a book that was lying open on the side
table. "*The Light Princess*. Mrs. Finchley, why is this book
here? It wasn't on my list."

"Sir, it's only to improve his imagination. His ability
to think."

Mr. Socrates' eyes narrowed. "Ability to think? If he
reads books for children he will remain a child." He handed
the book to her. "Have him read Shakespeare or Coleridge if
you must encourage flights of fancy. I thought I'd been clear
that any other books must first be vetted by me."

"They will be, sir."

Modo stared at his feet, ashamed that Mr. Socrates knew
he had been enjoying a child's book. *Am I acting too much
like a child?* he wondered.

Mr. Socrates turned back to Modo. "Tharpa certainly
praises your skill and strength. He claims you're an apt pupil."

Modo blushed.

"It has been four years since I rescued you. Four years
that you have spent in these three rooms, and you have been
extremely diligent in your training and your studies. I'm pleased
by your performance." He put his hand on Modo's shoulder.

Is this what fathers do? Modo wondered. Mr. Socrates wasn't his father, but he was the closest thing Modo had to one.

Mr. Socrates lifted his hand and looked at it as though he had surprised himself with the gesture. "You are well worth the investment, Modo. Now, would you like to see the outside world one day?"

"Yes. Yes!" Modo exclaimed, beaming. Then, catching himself, he replied with some restraint, "I would enjoy that very much, sir."

"Patience, Modo. That day will come soon enough. Today we have a different, more important lesson. But I must warn you, it will be a hard one."

"I don't understand," Modo said.

"Well, Modo, in all this time you have not seen your own reflection, have you."

Mrs. Finchley cleared her throat. "Mr. Socrates, I—"

"This is not an appropriate time to speak, Mrs. Finchley," he replied, without allowing his eyes to stray from Modo's face. "Before you meet the world, you must first know yourself. Do you understand?"

Modo looked from his teacher to his master and back again.

"Do you understand?"

Modo nodded hesitantly.

With that, Mr. Socrates pulled a small hand mirror from his vest pocket. On the back of it was depicted a royal lion inlaid with gold. The glittering mirror hypnotized Modo. Mr. Socrates turned the mirror slowly towards Modo's face.

Modo looked into the glass and saw, for the first time in his life, his own eyes blinking. One eye was larger than the other, protruding like an insect's. His enormous teeth were crooked. Bright red hair grew in clumps on his head. He had imagined his face as everything from beautiful to scarred and ugly, but this was much worse than he'd dreamed—uglier than any illustration he had ever seen. Disbelief turned to horror, and Modo's eyes grew wide and welled with tears.

He looked up at Mrs. Finchley and whispered, "You told me I was beautiful."

Collapsing on his knees, Modo slapped his hands over his eyes and wailed. He rolled into a weeping, moaning ball, his hump pressed against his shirt.

Mr. Socrates lowered the mirror. "I warned you that this would be a hard lesson. You are deformed. You are ugly. But remember this day, Modo. It's the day you learned that you've been given an incredible gift. Your unsightly countenance may seem unbearable now, but because of it, the world will always underestimate you. Natural selection has endowed you with a second gift, your capacity to change your deformed features, an ability that other men can only dream of. It is a most wonderful and valuable asset. Together, we will develop it."

Modo had stopped listening. The ghastly image of his face had been burned into his vision. He let out a sharp cry and beat at his head and his hump, as if to pound the abnormalities back into his flesh. He kicked so hard he propelled himself back into the wall, knocking plaster loose.

"Stop wailing!" Mr. Socrates commanded.

Modo tried to suppress his rasping. He calmed himself until he emitted only the occasional whimper, keeping his hands clamped over his face.

Slowly he looked up from the floor. Everyone's eyes were on him. Mrs. Finchley had been crying. Tharpa was, as always, unreadable, but Mr. Socrates, surprisingly, looked a little sad.

"I know you are only five but you must learn to control yourself," he whispered. "You must." He reached into the carpet bag at his feet and pulled out a flesh-coloured object.

Modo squinted at it, making out holes for eyes and a mouth.

"I ordered this especially for you, all the way from Venice. It is a mask. These masks are made from papier mâché, so they're very light. You'll hardly know you're wearing it." He set it on the floor beside Modo. It had a straight nose and perfectly formed lips.

Modo whimpered again.

Mr. Socrates turned away abruptly, saying, "Do not comfort him, Mrs. Finchley. That is an order. He must learn to accept his appearance. Let us leave the boy now. We shall have tea. I've brought a sample from the Tea Derby, fresh from Foochow."

And with that he strode to the door, Tharpa and Mrs. Finchley at his heels. She glanced back, but Modo hid his face again. Through his blubbering, he heard the door lock behind them.

After several seconds he lowered his hands, reached out and touched the mask. It was cold and hard. He picked it up and explored the eyeholes, the two smaller holes for his nostrils. He pushed the mask onto his face, pressed his back against the wall and wept.

CHAPTER 3

Learning to Be Untouchable

Sweat dripped into Modo's eyes as he climbed the rope to the skylight cupola. It was the twelfth time in the last hour that Tharpa had commanded him to "ascend with utmost speed." Modo paused at the top, held on with one hand and with the other rubbed at his latest mask. With Mrs. Finchley's help he'd constructed it from flour, water, paper pulp and glue. He'd given it a devilish, grinning face.

He leapt to a nearby rope, swung to the opposite wall and climbed down headfirst.

"You are strong for a child of nine years," Tharpa said in his formal English.

Modo grinned with pride. On the ground his gawky legs and awkward form were clumsy, but his large hands were made for climbing. He flipped over a sawhorse and landed on his feet. "Zounds!" he said.

Tharpa didn't react, so Modo flipped again. "Zounds!"

"Yes, yes, impressive," Tharpa said, but Modo couldn't tell if his instructor was mocking him. Although Modo had worked with Tharpa for five years, he still found the Indian completely unreadable.

Three days a week Tharpa would train Modo in what he called "the fighting arts." The rest of the week was spent reading history, learning languages and memorizing maps on which all the countries of the Empire were marked in red. As part of his schooling, he'd dress up in costumes with Mrs. Finchley, perfecting accents and pretending to be other people. Her years as an actress made her a fine teacher. And he assumed he was a fine student, for she praised him regularly.

Modo could now effortlessly list the order of precedence from Queen Victoria down to gentlemen allowed to bear arms, and explain who should be seated next to whom at a dinner party. Why Mrs. Finchley wanted him to know such trivial matters, he couldn't imagine.

Once a week, Mr. Socrates would visit carrying a photograph or a portrait which he'd set on an easel in front of Modo. "You must become this person," he'd say, and Modo, with all the willpower and imagination he could muster, would visualize his body shifting and the structure of his face changing, until, finally, painfully, his bones would actually move. More often than not, Modo failed to sustain the transformation, and moments later slipped back to his ugly self. But once in a while, he would shift his shape so completely that his eyebrows, nose and lips were similar to those of the person in the portrait, and he would manage to hold the look for as long as ten minutes.

On those rare days when Modo succeeded, Mr. Socrates would dole out a smattering of praise. Modo could feed on one passing "*That was satisfactory*" for a week, enthusiastically practising at night in bed, shifting his face, his shape, hoping to receive another compliment when next they met.

At one session, feeling brave, Modo asked, "Why do I have this ability?"

"Chameleons modify their colour according to their surroundings," Mr. Socrates explained. "Hares change their brown summer coat to white for the winter. I've seen species of fish that actually glow to hypnotize their prey. It's the perfect survival skill, Modo, to bewitch your enemies—to blend in with your friends. It's an adaptive transformation. Mother Nature has given you this gift."

Mr. Socrates kept calling it a gift. Modo wasn't so sure. He thought of the hours he'd spent changing his face and body, always reverting to his original form. Why couldn't he be changed forever? Mother Nature had been cruel to him.

He understood that a son should learn from his father. He had been told about being abandoned as a baby and that he had no father, but still he yearned for his master's attention. He wondered what Mr. Socrates did when he wasn't at Ravenscroft. Sometimes months would pass without the usual weekly visit and he'd explain his absence with a lesson, such as, "I was visiting Afghanistan. Point it out on the map."

He was away now, and had been for over a month, but Tharpa had arrived like clockwork to give lessons.

"You do not need to wear your mask for me, Modo," Tharpa said. "And you will not always be able to hide behind it when you fight."

Modo undid the knots and removed the mask, setting it on a table. He felt naked. This was not a face for the world to see; Mr. Socrates had told him so. At the master's insistence, Mrs. Finchley had long ago hung a mirror in the bedroom, yet Modo still had not grown used to his own reflection.

"Now, let us spar," Tharpa directed, and cracked his knuckles.

Modo raised his fists.

"Not boxing, nor savate." Tharpa reached for two long bamboo swords. "Kenjutsu."

He tossed Modo a sword and immediately swung at him, forcing him to parry. They moved side to side, slowly. The *tick* and *tack* rhythm was mesmerizing to Modo, so much so that he was completely surprised when Tharpa kicked at a small stool and sent it into Modo's knee.

"Anything can be a weapon, Modo. Even your own breath."

Modo laughed, but Tharpa looked quite serious. A second later he smiled.

"It depends on what you eat, of course. Garlic and onions: very dangerous."

This time Modo truly guffawed, and at that moment Tharpa swung a blow towards his head that Modo parried with ease.

"Laughter relaxes the muscles," Tharpa said. "Your technique is more natural now. Anger tightens them."

Modo struck back and Tharpa parried the blow.

"How long will I have to stay inside Ravenscroft?" Modo asked.

"Sahib will decide."

"Has he told you?"

"Sahib has not shared his plans with me."

Modo thought he saw an opening, so he snapped the sword down, but Tharpa turned it away. Modo watched his teacher's steady eyes.

"When you look at me you don't cringe," Modo said.

"There's no reason to," Tharpa answered.

Modo dodged to one side a moment too late; the bamboo slapped his shoulder, stinging him.

"Even Mr. Socrates recoils a little at the sight of me."

Tharpa shrugged and brought the sword down on Modo's leg.

"Ow!"

"No complaints," Tharpa said softly. "Expressing distress will only encourage the enemy." Then he stepped back, held up a hand and said, "The eyes see what the mind wants them to see."

"What do you mean?"

"I was invisible, once. I was born and raised in Bombay. I was a Dalit, an untouchable. My father was a carcass handler and he did not exist in the eyes of the upper castes. One day, he was struck by a wagon. No one would come to his aid as he lay there, so he died, and I was left alone. I could no longer bear to handle the dead bodies of animals so I joined the army and became Mr. Socrates' orderly. He recognized something in me. He said I had quickness of hand and spirit, but my past weighed too much on me, so he gave me a new name, to release me from my past. As Tharpa, I am no longer an untouchable Dalit. But he made me untouchable in a new way."

"Oh." Modo assumed Tharpa meant all the martial arts that he now taught.

"But I remember my past, young sahib. That is why I do not cringe when I see you. Your disfiguration, it is not your true self."

Modo would have smiled if Tharpa had not then struck him a glancing blow off his cheek.

"Hey, that's not fair. You raised your hand; I thought we were finished fighting."

"There is no 'fair,' Modo. No matter what you are doing your mind should not drift from the task of defending yourself. Your body must react no matter where your thoughts take you."

Modo nodded, his cheek stinging. It occurred to him then that Tharpa no longer had a father. And Modo did not know who his father was. This was something they shared.

Then another thought came to him: Mr. Socrates was father to both of them.

CHAPTER 4

Masterwork

Dr. Hyde sat at a large oak table strewn with gears, keys, small metal bones and two tiny marble eyes. Looking through a telescoping lens strapped over his left eye, he connected a silver wing to a metallic sparrow's body. Behind him, outside the mouth of the cave, palm trees waved in the wind. He didn't know the name of this island, even though he'd been living on it for over eight years.

He rarely ventured outside, avoiding the burning sun as much as possible. His food and all his scientific materials were brought to him by dark-skinned men and women in grass skirts. He looked at them curiously, wondering how to make them taller and stronger. As with all people their bones were weak; the human skeleton was such a poor design.

He still knew so little about those who employed him— only that their leader was called the Guild Master and that there were soldiers in the Guild's employ on the island too. The insignia on their grey uniforms was a clock face inside a triangle.

He tapped the wing with his finger, pleased to see it move smoothly up and down. The clockwork bird would be his newest pet. He still missed his hound, though. Magnus had been strengthened by the tincture, but age eventually had taken him. However, he had sired puppies, and, with the right alterations, Hyde had made them much more powerful and perfectly obedient. They were being used by the soldiers to patrol the island.

Three chimpanzees watched him guardedly from inside their iron cages. Two of the creatures had metal arms, the third a metal jaw and skull. Sticking out of each of their shoulders was an iron bolt.

Two cages were empty. A tinge of sadness struck Hyde when he glanced at them. He had been fond of both missing chimps, had even named them Isaac and Galilei, but a failed batch of the tincture had ended their lives rather brutally. From then on he stopped giving his subjects names.

He squinted at the three that were left. There was something in the way their cages were stacked, one on top of the next, that gave him pause. An idea began forming, but he dismissed it, determined to complete the task at hand. Perfecting the tincture for these cousins of humans was enough of a challenge for now and would require much more time and material. He marvelled at how easily his requests were filled; any chemical, any kind of metal, any substance he asked for was brought to him. Sometimes it would come a month later, but it would arrive.

He had mentioned to one of the soldiers that an assistant would be helpful, and three weeks later they delivered a Liverpool-raised boy named Griff. They had found him on a deserted island, half-starved. It hadn't taken the boy long to learn to follow Hyde's orders. His skin had turned yellow, though. Hyde noted that perhaps he shouldn't conduct experiments on his staff. It would be hard to find and train another assistant if the boy perished.

He placed both marble eyes in their sockets, and the sparrow suddenly seemed alive. Hyde unclipped the telescoping lens from his forehead and turned a key, winding the clockwork inside the bird. He set the sparrow down and it walked in a circle and chirped three times. Success!

A great *boom* sounded and Hyde looked up. It seemed to have come from the direction of the docks, several hundred yards away, down the hill and partly hidden from the cave by palm trees. He shuffled over to the doorway and saw that another steamship had docked. Steamships arrived every few days; it was nothing impressive.

He peered a bit farther along the beach and was pleased to see that the airship *Vesuvius* had docked at the large black iron tower, a massive floating grey cloud harnessed to the earth. He'd seen the dirigible Henri Giffard had used to fly from Paris to Trappes, but the *Vesuvius* was five times larger. The steam-powered propeller spun slowly. He was always impressed by the *Vesuvius*—it was as if he were seeing the future. Maybe a new shipment of powders had arrived.

After a few minutes, Dr. Hyde returned to his table and stroked the sparrow. As he did, he thought of the Society of Science in London. Those weak-minded men would be amazed at what he had accomplished in the past few years.

He still seethed when he thought of them and the parliamentarians who had branded him a scientific blasphemer.

"What are you dreaming about?"

The purr of her voice raised the hairs on the back of his neck. He turned towards the woman he knew only as Ingrid. His analytic mind wished he could measure the beats of his skipping heart and use that data to ascertain whether or not it was love. Oh, he was being foolish, again. Surely he was too old for love.

"What do I dream about?" he answered, and cleared his throat. "Oh, it's complex. Why just this morning I nearly had a wonderful idea, but I let it pass. Better to keep my mind on the tincture. I do see so many things of wonder, yet to be created."

"Like this?" she said, raising her arm. Her hook had been replaced by a gleaming metal hand. Her brass-hinged knuckles opened and closed quietly; even her golden fingernails were perfect.

My design, he thought, *added to her beauty*. She'd been stronger than any patient he'd ever encountered, keeping her trusting eyes open while he performed the operation, not once crying out as he attached piano wires to her tendons.

"Is it still functioning properly?"

She clicked her fingers together. "Yes, of course, thanks to you." She leaned forward and kissed his cheek. He felt himself go red.

"I'm coming so close to realizing the full potential of the tincture," he sputtered. At this, one of the chimpanzees let out a howl. Dr. Hyde locked eyes with the animal. They were even more intelligent than he had surmised. Maybe he could augment their jaws and tongue so they could speak. A new voice box? Would that—

"You were saying, Doctor?"

"Oh, yes, yes! The tincture is nearly ready for human consumption. And I have decided, after all these years, to give it a name: Lycaeunium."

"Ah, that is a clever name."

Hyde raised an eyebrow. "You know why I chose it?"

"I've read the Greek myths, dear Doctor. It can only be a reference to King Lycaon. He sacrificed a child to Zeus and was turned into a wolf."

"Well, then, you understand the reference. I do love my symbols. Lycaeunium turns creatures into stronger, more bestial versions of themselves. It seems there will be other uses too, which I am still investigating."

"The Guild Master will be pleased to know that."

"I have appreciated his assistance. Your support has allowed me to push past the limits of modern science. I possess a much greater understanding of the inner chemical workings of both the human and the animal brain."

"You must be very proud of yourself."

Her tone made him pause, but she gave him a guileless smile.

"I would like to know your thoughts," he said. "Are we just the sum of the chemical reactions in the brain? Or is there more? Is there—as a man of science I hesitate to say this—a spirit in us that can be tapped into?"

"Of course. It is our will to live. What it can be used for, I imagine, is boundless."

He nodded. "I believe I've found a way to access this energy."

"The Guild Master celebrates your every success."

"When will I finally meet him?" Dr. Hyde asked.

"In time, I suppose, if it's necessary." She stroked the wing of the sparrow and it let out a little *cheep*. "Very pretty. Will you make one for me?"

"Of course! Anything!" He caught his breath. "Within reason, of course."

She tapped her metal fingers against her cheek. "I am always reasonable. And your sparrow reminds me, I do have a new, secondary project for you." She made a motion with her good hand and four soldiers rose from where they'd been hiding in the foliage outside the cave. They marched in carrying a lumpy object on a stretcher.

"What's this?" Dr. Hyde asked, startled, and as they rolled the object off the stretcher onto his operating table, he couldn't restrain a shudder. The thing they carried was a man with no arms and no legs. His dark hair and beard were matted and his eyes closed.

"This is a valuable member of the Guild. I wonder if you could repair him."

"Repair him?" Dr. Hyde watched the man's chest slowly rise and fall. "How—how is it that he still lives?"

"Oh, an infusion into his bloodstream of some sugars. We have other doctors in our employ. He does wake occasionally to eat and to swear. Be prepared for that. He has a temper."

"What's his name?"

"You don't need to know a man's name in order to oper-
ate on him, do you?"

"No, you're right. But I—I—"

"Say no more. I have faith that you will find a way to help
him. I will consider the matter closed." She made another
gesture, and the soldiers turned as one and left the cave.

"And the question I asked when I first walked in was
not an idle one," she said. "You have done so much for
the Guild. It is time we repaid you. Is there something you
dream of constructing?"

He was frozen, his mind still in shock. He stared at the
new patient. How could he possibly put that man back
together?

"Pay attention to me, Cornelius."

The doctor looked at her; she was smiling. "You have
such a wandering mind. The Guild Master, like you, loves
his symbols. He generously offers you all of our resources to
create a masterwork."

"A masterwork?" He looked at his sparrow, at the flasks
that held the tincture and finally at the chimpanzees in their
cages. In a flash his earlier idea became completely clear to
him.

"Yes," Hyde said slowly. "Yes. I imagine a device. A
weapon unlike any ever used before."

CHAPTER 5

The First Assignment

Tharpa opened the door to Modo's room, carrying a bag of travelling clothes. It was Modo's thirteenth year of living in Ravenscroft and his fourteenth year of life.

"Dress, please." Tharpa tossed the bag to Modo. The clothes inside weren't fashionable, nor well threaded in the style of Mr. Socrates. They were coarse and loose-fitting like those worn by the lower classes. Modo had dressed up in similar costumes while play-acting with Mrs. Finchley. He pulled on a pair of worn grey breeches, a thick shirt and a coat with large bone buttons. Then he squeezed his splayed feet into a pair of hobnailed boots. Finally, Tharpa placed a camlet cloak over Modo's shoulders. When the hood was pulled up over his head in just the right way, it hid his features. He snapped it off and back on three times, then froze with it over his face until Tharpa stepped up to peek in at him.

"Boo!" Modo shouted, flicking off the hood.

Tharpa gave a wry smile. Nothing unnerved the man.

Mr. Socrates marched briskly into the room, his walking stick tap-tap-tapping across the marble floor. It was topped with a cobalt-blue glass knob that Modo thought looked magical. Mr. Socrates peered down at Modo, rolling the stick back and forth between his palms.

"In a few minutes we shall be taking the carriage to Lincoln. Then we catch the London train," he said, as though it were just another day.

"London!" Modo had read so much about it. There would be bridges, Madame Tussauds wax museum, Queen Victoria and Trafalgar Square. The thought of going outside, of seeing the green trees and breathing the fresh air, of visiting London, made Modo want to burst out clapping and shouting, but he knew better than to behave in such an inappropriate manner in front of Mr. Socrates. He clasped his hands tightly under his cloak.

"London," he said stiffly, "how very interesting."

Outside. With the rest of the world. Where there were princes and queens, shoemakers and jugglers. Imagine seeing a play or a musical troupe! Imagine standing in a crowd. That gave Modo pause. Would people be horrified at the sight of him? Outside everything was new and possibly dangerous. He peeked around at the familiar rooms. It had always been safe here.

Mr. Socrates had been observing him. "You hesitate?"

"No, sir." He had hoped his voice would sound more confident.

"On our journey you shall behave like a second servant— for that you are dressed appropriately."

"I won't let you down. I promise, sir."

"Then follow me."

Mr. Socrates left the room, and Modo glanced at Tharpa, who nodded. The new boots were awkward and heavy. Modo nearly tripped over his own feet as he walked towards the open door. He snatched up his mask as he passed the dresser.

He'd occasionally glimpsed the kitchen through the door to his rooms as Mrs. Finchley went to and fro, but he'd never been on the other side of the door. For the first time in twelve years he stepped out of the only rooms he'd ever known. In the kitchen his eyes darted from the cast-iron stove crowded with tin pots to the rows of knives and the hanging wooden and metal spoons. The kitchen was marvellously interesting—and he wasn't even outside yet!

Mr. Socrates tugged his shoulder, and Modo followed him down a hallway, avoiding his reflection in a large oval mirror. But next to it was a painting of an earl or a lord or someone of noble mien. He looked a little like Mr. Socrates.

"Who's that?" Modo asked.

"The past," Mr. Socrates said. "Best to leave it behind. Now hurry." He was standing in the open front door.

Modo tried to charge by him, but Mr. Socrates whipped his walking stick across the door to block it. Modo cowered.

"For heaven's sake, boy, put your mask on," Mr. Socrates snapped. "No one should see your face."

Modo dropped his head in shame, lifted his mask from his belt, placed the cold papier mâché across his face and tightened the strings behind his head. This one was flesh-coloured with a small nose.

"Few people wear masks, Modo. Only those with serious burns or facial disfigurations. You're too young to be a wounded veteran, so if anyone asks, tell them it was a boiler accident."

"I will, sir."

He followed Mr. Socrates out of Ravenscroft and into the green yard, past a well-tended flower garden. "Cowslip," he whispered at the yellow flowers. Mrs. Finchley had brought them into the house on occasion. "They grow right here. And *Epimediums*!" He leaned down to touch the white petals and breathe in their scent.

A loud snort disturbed the quiet of the morning and Modo looked up. In the lane stood a carriage, four horses intermittently stamping their hooves. Horses! They were so much bigger than he had imagined. He wanted to pat their sides. A pigeon flitted in the air, drawing his attention, and for a moment he stared right at the sun. The sky seemed to stretch forever. He shook his head, blinked and focused on the decaying gazebo, vines criss-crossing its latticed walls.

Mrs. Finchley waited near the laneway, fidgeting with her apron. He leapt across the lawn towards her.

"Outside! I'm outside!"

"You've had to wait a long time," she said sadly.

Modo frowned behind his mask. "Yes—yes, I have."

"You are a good boy," she whispered. "A good, sweet boy. Never forget that."

He grinned and bowed to her, saying, "Oh, you are far too kind."

"Come along, Modo," Mr. Socrates called. He was

already seated in the carriage, checking his pocket watch. "Mrs. Finchley, we cannot be detained any longer."

She gently lifted the mask and stroked Modo's cheek. He put his hand on hers. "I shall truly miss you, Modo," she said. Her eyes filled with tears. "I'll keep you in my prayers."

Modo squeezed her hand. "Why are you upset? I'll see you soon."

She said nothing.

Modo swallowed. "I will, won't I?"

"Of course," she said, but she wouldn't meet his eyes.

"Modo. Come now!" Mr. Socrates shouted.

She grabbed both his hands and held them tight. "Go on, Modo. You're strong. And you *are* beautiful, remember that. It has been a privilege to teach you." She took a step back, then walked up the path to the house, wiping her face with a handkerchief.

Modo watched her for a moment, his heart aching. Then he pulled down the mask, plodded to the carriage and reached for the handrail.

"No," Mr. Socrates chided. "A servant rides beside the driver."

Modo climbed up and sat on the narrow bench next to Tharpa, who flicked the reins until the four horses began trotting. Modo turned and waved madly at Mrs. Finchley, who stood at the door of Ravenscroft, one hand covering her mouth, the other waving limply.

He lifted his mask and wiped at his eyes with his sleeve, then peeped at Tharpa, who, thankfully, had been too busy with the horses to pay Modo any attention. Modo couldn't allow himself such sadness. He would see Mrs. Finchley again; he'd make sure of it.

They travelled without speaking. Modo's eyes, watering in the breeze, darted everywhere, trying to take in every tree, stone and field as they passed it. His ears echoed with the snorts of the horses and the melodies of birds. Birds! The carriage moved so fast that the ground blurred, making him dizzy if he looked down at it for too long. His stomach churned and he gripped the seat tightly.

Soon farmers in their carts joined them on the road, as did other carriages. Tharpa pulled on the reins until the horses slowed down. When they dropped manure, Modo laughed uncontrollably until Tharpa gave him a frown.

After another hour they were at the outskirts of a city where people carrying baskets walked along the side of the road. Costermongers, Modo knew from the books he'd read. Out to sell their vegetables and fruits. One girl gave him a curious glance and Modo pulled the cowl of his cloak farther over his face and touched his mask to be certain it was tight.

"Where are we?" he asked. "Is this London?"

Tharpa chuckled. "No, young Modo, this is just Lincoln."

They passed by a castle so enormous that Modo could only gape. The books he had memorized were coming to life before his very eyes, but the pictures had been so deceptively small. A maid lugged an overstuffed clothing bag up the hill, followed by a woman in a fine blue dress and a portly man using a walking stick. Everywhere he looked someone new popped up, more people than he could possibly count.

Soon they stopped at the train station and Modo caught

his first breathtaking glimpse of a steam train; the iron beast dwarfed the clumps of passengers. He helped unload the luggage. Then Tharpa took the carriage to the nearby liveries, while Modo carried the luggage, following his master, playacting the dutiful servant. He stared at the train, counted eight cars and an engine. Mr. Socrates purchased three first-class tickets and led Modo through the lines of people to the first car, where a private compartment awaited them.

The door was polished mahogany with a silver latch. Modo opened it so that Mr. Socrates could enter. Once Modo had dragged in the luggage, he sat on the cushioned seat across from Mr. Socrates and gawked out the window. Men, women, children drifted through the mist exhaled by the steam engine as if they were walking out of a magical world. No one looked at him—maybe they couldn't see through the glass. Minutes later Tharpa arrived and settled next to Modo.

A powerful, long whistle blasted as the train lurched forward and began to chug, causing Modo to shiver with excitement. The train seemed alive, pulling all its weight down the tracks. Modo had always been interested in steam power and had read as much as he could about it, begging Mr. Socrates and Mrs. Finchley to bring him more books on the subject. Steam engines powered locomotives and steamships all across the British Empire. It was amazing, really.

Modo imagined the fireman feeding coal into the firebox, the heat driving the vapours through the steam chest, pushing the giant piston and pulling the train along.

"How much force would it take to pull this train?" Mr. Socrates asked.

Modo counted on his fingers. How many passenger cars were there? Eight. He'd been trained to keep track of details. He busied himself calculating how much tractive effort it would take. How much would a train engine weigh? A passenger car? He could only guess. Then there were the people.

"It would take an eighty-thousand-pound force to pull this train, Mr. Socrates," he said.

"Good work, Modo. I remain impressed by your mathematical skills."

Modo began to fiddle absentmindedly with his mask.

"Keep your mask on in case a valet stops by," Mr. Socrates said. "You must remember what you are now, Modo. I've warned you. It may mean life or death."

Life or death? Modo dropped his hands and sank back into his seat. *What could that possibly mean?* Beside him, Tharpa was leaning back, looking out the window.

The train had reached its top speed. Modo watched the world blur in the window. He'd thought the carriage fast, but this was like travelling on a bullet. He grew queasy trying to keep his eyes on the scenery.

Mr. Socrates handed him a paper. "I have the latest edition of the *Times*. You may read it while we travel."

Modo took it happily. He'd read countless editions, always days or weeks old, but here he was, on a train to London, reading the *Times*. Today's paper!

On the first page was an article about a bill being passed

in Parliament and another about Siberian mammoth tusks arriving at the docks. He was wonderstruck at the illustrations. Below that was a short notice that a man's body had been found in the Thames. Modo wondered how the man had died. He turned the page, hoping to learn more, but his eyes were drawn to a new headline: "Wolf-Boy Discovered in Regent's Park."

> At Marylebone in Regent's Park, Henry Carr, a carpenter, was walking and heard what he described as a loud growl. Upon further inspection he discovered in the trees a young boy, who was naked and dirty. The boy spoke no words and could only snarl. Mr. Carr was able to subdue the feral child and deliver him into custody. He has since been identified as one of the orphans who have been declared missing from their orphanages. He was examined by Doctor Severn, who reported a perplexing discovery. The boy had several clean cuts along his shoulders, recently stitched together by someone with expertise. Who did this, and why, remains a mystery.

Modo touched his own shoulder, felt the edge of his hump. He wished a surgeon could remove it. Did the young boy in the article feel as unsightly as Modo did? Is that what drove him to become feral?

He looked up from the paper to find Mr. Socrates staring at him.

"So tell me, Modo, what have you been reading?"

Modo sucked in a breath, the air whistling between his crooked teeth. He was about to be tested.

"Mammoth tusks have arrived in London."

Mr. Socrates nodded. "Geologically interesting. What else?"

"Uh, Parliament passed a bill about . . ." His voice trailed off.

"They are always passing bills while others do the hard work of running this country. That's not news."

"A body was discovered in the Thames," Modo offered.

"Tragic but common enough—there are over three million souls in London: you can't expect them all to behave in a civilized manner. Did anything else in the paper catch your eye?"

"A wolf-boy was found in the park."

"Yes, *that* was a curious item. What would cause such a condition in a young boy? I wonder. Was his regression natural? Or was he the foster child of some wild beast? The way in which a child is raised will stay with him for life."

Modo now saw what the lesson was. "Thank you for raising me properly."

Mr. Socrates chuckled. "I wasn't looking for a compliment, Modo."

"Oh . . . well . . . why did the child have stitches?"

"That, I cannot say. There are men in London who have unsavoury minds. The poor child must have been captured by one of them." He paused. "I assume you feel some kinship with the boy. After all, you are an oddity like him. Many would look at you and be frightened or disgusted.

That's why I insisted on the mask."

Modo's gut began to churn. If Londoners saw his real face would they think he was the offspring of an animal?

"I have invested a great deal of thought into your upbringing and education. You must wonder what my purpose is." Mr. Socrates leaned forward as though he were about to reveal a tantalizing secret.

Modo had thought about that very thing nearly every day for years, but he said, "It wasn't my place to ask."

Mr. Socrates rubbed his chin. "Perhaps you are too meek. Even Tharpa has learned to challenge me from time to time."

Modo looked at Tharpa, who raised his eyebrows as if to say this was a revelation to him as well.

"It is imperative that you understand how complicated the world is. What you read in the paper is what many would call 'reality.' But under those stories about governments or murders are layers of meaning. When you read about a body found in the Thames, is it just another drunkard stabbed for his pocket watch? Or is it a secret agent prevented from accomplishing his task?"

"You think that man was a secret agent?" Modo exclaimed, now on the edge of his seat.

"Perhaps. Organizations exist whose sole purpose is to undermine everything we British are doing to make the world a better place."

"Organizations?"

"Every country, enemy or ally, has its spies. We must vigilantly guard against them all."

Modo shot another look at Tharpa, hoping to receive confirmation of what Mr. Socrates had said, but Tharpa continued to gaze out at the blurring fields of green.

"Don't worry your head about it now," Mr. Socrates said. "You'll have your place in the struggle. We shall learn soon enough whether or not your training was worth the investment."

"What do you mean?"

"We'll discuss it later. Let's just say I have an assignment for you. Now, please carry on with your reading."

Modo opened the paper again, but he couldn't read a word. An assignment! His mind was buzzing with possibilities. Over the years Mr. Socrates had hinted that all his instruction was for an important, undisclosed purpose. Now Modo knew. He was to battle these secret organizations. His mouth felt dry with fright.

It was well past sundown when they pulled into London. Gas lights flickered here and there as figures scurried along a platform, cutting through the steam belched by the train.

"Come, Modo," Mr. Socrates said, getting to his feet. "Paddington Station. We shall disembark here. Bring the luggage."

As he stepped off the train with Mr. Socrates' suitcase in hand, Modo couldn't believe his eyes. There were even more people at this station than at the one in Lincoln, and they were bleating, squawking, shouting, all speaking at once. A woman who must have bathed in perfume waddled by, her flower scent invading his nostrils. He clutched the suitcase to his chest and hurried to catch up with Mr. Socrates.

Modo glanced up from time to time to see if people were

staring at him and his mask, but they were too busy to notice him. It was all Modo could do to keep from dropping the suitcase and running away from the hurly-burly.

They stopped on a street where tall, soot-blackened buildings were obscured by smoke and fog. Mr. Socrates raised his hand and the clomping of hooves echoed off the nearby walls. A large coach charged out of the mist, its driver dressed in a white mackintosh that made him look like a wraith.

"You'll ride with me now," Mr. Socrates instructed Modo. Tharpa took the seat up top beside the driver.

As the horses clopped down the street, Modo peered out the window. The spectral forms of Londoners swirled up the alleys.

"You've displayed an admirable capacity for tutelage," Mr. Socrates said. "I'm pleased. Mrs. Finchley would say I've been hard on you, but I have my reasons."

"Yes, sir."

"Modo, there's an important assignment you must complete. It is my sincere hope that all your training, all your diligent studying will result in a successful mission, for it will be, as they say, a sink or swim situation."

"I don't understand, sir," Modo croaked.

"Now you must survive on the streets of London . . . on your own."

It took a few moments for the words to sink in. "On my own?"

"Exactly." Mr. Socrates thumped the roof with his walking stick. The coach slowed, then stopped. "This assignment is intended to cut the apron strings. You have been an exceptional student, but it is time that you learn to act independently." Mr. Socrates swung open the door.

"You want me to . . . leave?"

"Please, Modo, don't belabour the obvious. Prove that my investment in you is well-founded. I'll find you again when you have completed your assignment. Go, at once."

Hesitantly Modo stepped down onto the wet street.

"Wh-wh-when will you come for me? How long will—"

Mr. Socrates closed the door. From his perch next to the driver, Tharpa refused to look at Modo. The driver cracked his whip and the horses trotted on, while Modo shouted from the curb, "But wait! I have no food! No money! Mr. Socrates! I need my clothes! Tharpa! Wait!"

Modo watched, stunned, as the coach turned down an alley and was gone. He stared after it for a long time as though at any moment it would reappear and his nightmare would be over. His heart thumped madly. He breathed in and out. Inside the coach, he'd felt safe, accustomed as he was to having walls around him. Here on the street with the sky open above him and the freedom to choose any direction he liked, Modo felt confused and uncertain.

And then, from behind him, a voice cut through the fog.

"'Ere's a pritty lad. Come'n let me see yeh."

Modo spun around, and then leapt back in fright. A dead horse stared blankly from the back of a knacker wagon. From around the other side lurched an old woman, her eyes glazed with madness. A smile twisted her chapped lips, revealing black broken teeth.

"Come 'ere, laddie," she rasped, reaching for him with gnarled hands. "Why you wearin' a mask? Let me 'ave it."

Modo stumbled, caught himself on a lamp post, then, in a frenzy, ran down one cobblestone street after another, deeper into the city.

CHAPTER 6

Secret Life

Six months later a letter arrived at the Langham Hotel. The bellman slid it under the door of room 443, where it was picked up by a young, but slightly callused hand. The letter was read once, its contents committed to memory, then it was burned.

Octavia Milkweed chose a blue bonnet and matching dress with a crinoline, applied a light dusting of rouge to hide her freckles and used the hotel pen and ink to write down the name of a man and his address. The ink was a cheap kind and she had to go over her writing twice. She waited for the note to dry before placing it in her purse, then left the room, umbrella in hand. She rode the lift down to the lobby and had the porter hail a Hansom cab. Moments later the driver helped her up the steps to her seat. When she told him their destination, he furrowed his wide brow.

"Seven Dials? Are you certain?" he asked.

"I am always certain," she replied with a degree of haughtiness.

The cabbie shook his head. She felt the cab jerk and shake as he climbed into his station at the back and flicked the reins. The horse trotted down the granite-paved street.

Octavia grinned. She knew that being confident and dressing in such finery intimidated lower-class men. The cabbie probably thought she was twenty years old. Maybe even twenty-five. Her own best guess at her real age was that she was fifteen. No one had written down her birthdate at the orphanage, so she would never know for certain.

She had rehearsed the instructions in the letter several times, creating both a new persona and a plan. Acting had always come naturally. She hadn't much liked being herself, most of her childhood years. Better to invent someone new.

It was still light out when they drove through Seven Dials. It was a nasty neighbourhood, and Octavia knew it well. Seven streets met at a junction with a sundial in the centre. She'd eaten and drunk in the gin shops and pubs, hidden in a cellar nearby to avoid Picklenose, a particularly nasty copper. Any of the ragged children, with their dirty hands pressed up against shop windows displaying third-hand dresses, could have been her a few years before. Even the sundial brought back memories: it was the first place she'd kissed a boy, a young gentleman. She had stolen his watch and wallet that day. A good haul.

Two horses snorted as they pulled an omnibus past Octavia's cab, clerks in derby hats gawking out the windows; below them was emblazoned an advertisement for Oakey's Knife Polish. The omnibus nearly collided with a knacker wagon. She wondered what madman had designed such an intersection. Ruffians ran in front of her cab, paying no mind to the danger presented by horse hooves. She directed the cabbie to a nearby pub.

"Please, hurry and do your errand, madam," said the cabbie. "These streets ain't safe."

She offered him threepence. "This will ease your mind." He coughed gently into his gloved hand and she dropped a few more coins into his palm.

When she entered the Red Boar a cloud of odours of burned bread, burped beer and thick smoke made her wrinkle up her nose in disgust. The pub was lit by one large oil lamp. Three customers, already sodden, were slumped against a table. One lifted red-rimmed eyelids to take her in. She told the portly innkeeper her purpose, giving him her kindest smile.

"Oh, you want to see Mr. W, do you?" the innkeeper grumbled. "He's rooming at the top of the stairs. Oppie, show our guest the way."

Octavia thought the man was speaking to the air, until a pile of rags behind the counter moved. A dirty-faced boy, body thin as a broomstick, rubbed at his eyes, yawned and stood up.

"Be quick!" the innkeeper barked.

"This way, missus," the boy said, leading her through a door and up a set of creaking stairs.

"You got business wif Mr. W?" he asked.

She judged him to be no more than eight. The only clean thing on him was a near-fashionable red neckerchief tied over his collar.

"Yes, I do. Though I must admit I have never met him. What is he like?"

"I brings 'im 'is meal free times a day when I'm not cleaning out the slop for Mr. Berks. Sometimes Mr. W tells me stories. 'E reads 'em from a book."

"So he lets you into his room?"

"No. I ent never seen 'im. 'E reads 'em through the door. 'E's a brainy sort—a master detective, 'e is. Find anyfing or anyun vat's missing, one 'undred percentages guaranteed. 'E's better van all 'em clowns in Scotland Yard."

"How much does he pay you to say that?" she asked kindly.

"Ma'am! God's truth, I'm just repeating what I 'ear on the street. 'E's a real good sort. And 'e says I could one day be 'is 'prentice. Oppie Wilkers, Detective. Nice ring, ent it? 'E's generous, too. 'E gave me vis neckerchief, when I told 'im it was me birfday."

"And was it your birthday?"

"Of course, miss. Of course!"

Octavia nodded. The boy was lying. She'd changed her own birthdate on occasion to coax gifts out of unsuspecting boys. The kid was clever, but talkative. The bit about Mr. W never opening his door was an interesting piece of information. He must be a very private man.

She was led up a narrow staircase where a small broken window let in a few rays of light.

"'At's where Mr. W stays. Top o' the inn, it is. Only room up 'ere." He pointed at a door. "I leaves 'is meals 'ere. 'E's partial to chicken." On the floor was a plate littered with bones. Oppie picked it up. "Wot else you need, missus?"

"That will be all." She slipped twopence into his hand and he gave her a near-toothless grin.

"Be at your beck 'n' call just down the stairs," he exclaimed as he skipped away.

Octavia stood in front of Mr. W's door and noted the lion that had been carved into it. She considered the stature of the guests who may at one time have stayed there.

She knocked and waited, but there was no reply, which gave her pause. The letter hadn't said what to do in the event that her contact was unavailable. Perhaps she should leave a note. Then, just as she was about to call for Oppie, she heard the groan of floorboards.

"Yes?" asked a deep, male voice from the other side of the door.

"I have come about your notice in the paper. I need you to find something."

A few moments passed. "What sort of item?"

She sensed he was not using his real voice. The pitch occasionally wavered.

"A very important one. May I come in, Mr. . . . Mr. . . . ?"

"Mr. Wellington."

"Wellington? Truly?"

"Yes. But I'm not the Duke of Wellington, obviously. And no, you may not come in. Those who employ me cannot see me."

"Then how will I know I can trust you?"

"Never trust your eyes, that's my motto. In any case, by remaining anonymous I can move around London Town and beyond without being recognized. If you don't agree with the terms you are free to go. But you should know I have many satisfied customers."

He spoke with a slight accent; she couldn't place it. His tone was sombre and each word deliberate.

A flicker of light on the door drew her attention. She now saw that a tiny peephole had been rigged in the eye of the carved lion.

"Mr. Wellington," she said wryly, "are you watching me?"

A *thud* from the other side of the door. "No. Don't be silly. I can't see through doors."

Knowing full well he could see her, she resisted the urge to smile.

"Well, then, if those are your terms I suppose I have no choice but to accept them. And since this mission is of utmost importance, you must begin today."

"Today? I am rather busy, of course, but, well . . . What is it you want me to find?"

"It will no doubt sound peculiar, but you see, the thing I have lost is . . . my brother." The floorboards on the other side of the door creaked and she imagined him scratching his head.

"Your brother?"

"Yes. My dear brother."

"Has he left the country? Does he gamble?"

"Forgive me. I haven't been clear. My brother's not gone, exactly. I see him every day. But it's . . . at night."

She touched her hand to her forehead as though she were about to faint. The door jiggled on its hinges.

"At night he disappears," she whispered. "He's a member of the Young Londoners Exploratory Society. He says he's only attending meetings, but sometimes he returns looking crazed and . . . Mr. Wellington?"

"Yes."

"Once I saw blood on his clothing."

"His own blood?"

"He says it was a nosebleed, but I worry. He is, I don't know . . . not himself. Sometimes I feel as though I've lost him."

Octavia pulled a lace handkerchief from her sleeve. Its corner was monogrammed with a large *L*. She dabbed her eyes.

"There, there. Please don't cry. I will do my best to discover the source of your brother's difficulties."

"So you'll take on the case?" she said breathlessly.

"Yes, but first I do have an important question. What is your name?"

"Audrette Featherstone," she said with a sniffle.

"Well, Miss Featherstone, please be so kind as to give me more details about your brother, beginning with a physical description, a list of his habits and what he does during the day. Oh, and where he lives."

"I have his address here." She bent down and slid the note she had prepared under the door. She glimpsed a gloved finger as Mr. Wellington snatched the paper from the other side. She heard him clear his throat.

"Good. Good. Allow me a moment to fetch my journal."

Octavia smiled. She had completed her assignment. Her employer would be pleased.

CHAPTER 7

Rooftop Pursuit

A cloud of cold mist hung over London's rooftops and drizzled onto Modo's back. His large wet hands were clamped around the edge of the roof and he stared down on the city like a gargoyle, rarely blinking. Drops collected on his wide brow and trickled down his face, dripping off his crooked nose. Tharpa had taught him how to remain completely still, even to slow his heart rate.

The mask hanging from his belt was black—his night mask. He didn't wear it unless he had to because when he was jumping from rooftop to rooftop it would sometimes slip and cover his eyes. The night he had nearly smashed his skull open on a crossbeam he learned a valuable lesson.

Directly below, flickering gas lights cast odd shadows across a courtyard. A figure in a frock coat appeared on the far side of the yard and walked towards him. As the figure got closer his pale face became clear. Modo cracked a thin smile. He'd been following Oscar Featherstone for over an hour, from his home in Highgate to this rooftop above the fancy shops and row houses of Marylebone. When Oscar caught a cab in Highgate, Modo had been forced to leap from roof to roof in pursuit, working up a terrible sweat.

Now Oscar walked past him and through an archway. Modo froze for a few more moments, then scrambled across the shingles, his short bow legs surprisingly well-suited to the steep slopes and changing angles. He leapt, his haversack swinging at his shoulder, and landed near the top of another roof, grasping a lightning rod to steady himself. A startled pigeon flew into the fog.

His target was walking down an alley, so Modo bounded silently alongside and above him, stifling a chuckle. The young gentleman had no idea he was being trailed.

Ever since Mr. Socrates dropped him in the middle of London, Modo had learned to use rooftops to his advantage. In the first frightening minutes after the carriage had pulled away, he scampered down several streets, darted through crowds and, finally, startled by the sight of a miserable drunk and his vicious dog, leapt up to a rooftop and huddled in a recess. From there he watched the day unfold. When night fell again, he crept across the shingles, lapping up grey water from an eavestrough and reaching through a window to steal a pork pie.

By the third day he was confident enough to return to the street, shifting his face into that of a handsome young man. He helped lift a carriage stuck in deep septic mud and received a penny for his trouble. Soon he found other jobs that required his unusual strength. He slept in Hyde Park at night, until the police shooed him off, then he moved to a manure-rich stable. He squirreled his money away until he could afford at least a lice-infested room and a hot meal.

At night he would take to the rooftops and watch the Londoners: the furtive movements of young ruffians who pickpocketed gentlemen on their way to the opera; women with impossible hats and beautiful faces out for tea; bobbies on their patrols, clutching their truncheons; brawlers shouting near the pubs. On the roofs of London he was safe and he could observe much more than most anyone else in the city.

Once he watched a lower-class family walk to church. Their shabby clothes, shoes and tired eyes made him wonder if he was lucky to have been raised in Ravenscroft. *Did Mr. Socrates save me from this sort of pauper life?* he asked himself. But when the father put a hand on the son's shoulder, a lump rose in Modo's throat.

It was a dog that had led him down the path to his current work as a detective. From a rooftop, he'd spotted a trim white hound with an ornate collar. It had leapt a low wall and was trapped in a blind alley. Modo heard the dog's owner call for it. Modo dropped down to the alley and, thankfully, found the dog to be friendly. He still smiled when he recalled how it had licked his hand. He led it to its master and was paid threepence.

He was inspired to place small notices in the *Times*, advertising "Lost Things Found" under the name Wellington. He thought people would trust the name. The Duke of Wellington had been a war hero, after all. Soon there were many requests for his services, people needing help to find everything from the mundane (wallets and walking canes) to the curious (a highly praised violin and a wooden leg). In a matter of weeks he was able to move into the Red Boar, taking a room on the top floor with a coal stove and easy access to the roof.

He'd spent nearly every night of the past six months on these rooftops. They belonged to him now, and were the only place he felt free. He had each dormer and slanting surface memorized. He could get from his room to Trafalgar Square faster than any cab. And what made it all so easy was that Londoners never looked up; they were always watching the cobblestones or hunching under umbrellas.

But tonight, as he trailed Oscar Featherstone across Baker Street, Modo sensed he had moved up in the world. In this assignment he felt a certain prestige. No more searching for lost wallets. Now he was on a *case*; he was a real detective. This is what he'd been trained for.

It had been relatively simple to follow Oscar from his manor. The real test would be whether or not he could uncover what had been keeping the man up so late at night and frightening his sister so.

His sister.

Audrette.

The thought of her name made Modo feel warm on a cold night, and yes, even giddy. She was so lovely, and spoke with angelic eloquence. He pictured the way she'd dabbed at her eyes with the handkerchief. He had memorized the moment, so tragic, sad, and at the same time so beautiful. His heart began racing uncomfortably and he nearly lost his grip on the shingles.

"Don't get addled, Modo," he whispered angrily at himself, adjusting his haversack so that it sat squarely on his humped back.

He crept along the rooftop until Oscar turned off the street and passed through an iron gate. At a two-storey brick house, he knocked on the door. The silhouette of the person who answered filled the door frame, so Modo deduced it was a man. The hulking figure stepped aside so that Oscar could enter the house. The door closed.

Modo surveyed the area. The roof of the house was too high and too far away for him to swing onto it. The stone wall surrounding the yard wasn't in good shape, sections crumbling here and there. But between him and the house, in the middle of the yard, sat an old gazebo that would likely support his weight.

Modo ran quietly to the edge of the rooftop and launched himself towards the gazebo, taking a few branches off the oak tree as he flew through the air. He landed on the structure's rounded roof with a *thud* and immediately bounced from there to a large balcony directly above the front door of the house.

He'd tried to land lightly, but he'd made far too much noise all the same, so he hid in the corner next to the drain-pipe and waited until he was sure no one would come out looking. Tharpa would have been proud to see how he was putting his teachings into practice. Except, perhaps, for that last jump.

He padded to the edge of the balcony and removed his bendable spyglass from his haversack. It had taken great patience and many hours to create the instrument, reshaping and joining two spyglasses with his large-knuckled, fumbling fingers. He extended his invention and put the eyepiece up to his right eye. Then he lowered the other end over the side of the balcony until he was looking into a dirty windowpane. The angle wasn't perfect and the fish-eye lens distorted the view even more. Nonetheless, soon Modo got his bearings and slowly scanned the room. He could make out Oscar talking to a man who had his back to the window. The man was tall, his immense shoulders stuffed into a suit coat, his hair black as coal. Modo watched them until the man walked away from the window, opened a door and ushered Oscar into another room out of Modo's sight.

Now the best way to find out what Oscar was up to would be to get inside the house. He could easily break in through the balcony door, but he had no idea what, or who, was on the other side. It would be much more logical to walk in through the front door. That would require a transformation. He backed up into the corner of the balcony again.

You will always be ugly, Mr. Socrates had regularly reminded him over the years. *Always. But you are better able to adapt than any chameleon. Be thankful for it.*

At the moment Modo was feeling anything but thankful as he checked his pocket watch and turned his will to altering his body. Fire burned in his veins as his bones shifted in their sockets. He'd performed this "adaptive transformation," as Mr. Socrates called it, thousands of times. He had worked to perfect each change.

He closed his eyes, grimacing, picturing the man he wanted to look like. He chose an appearance inspired by a sketch of Peterkin, a favourite character from the novel *The Coral Island*. Mrs. Finchley had allowed him to read it, but he had to promise to hide the book whenever Mr. Socrates visited. Modo's facial plates shifted and became angular, his skin stretching smoothly across his new skull and straightened nose.

His arms became thinner and longer, his chest smaller. And finally he turned his will to the hump, the dreadful hump. He forced it to sink into his flesh.

He picked up his pocket watch. Three minutes. Mr. Socrates would have been pleased.

Sweating and tired, Modo patted his face to be sure he hadn't missed any unsightly lumps. He could hold this shape for only five hours, at the most. Then his muscles would grow weak and he'd slip back into his natural, repulsive self.

His clothing looked ridiculous on his new thin frame, so he took another cautious look around and stripped to his underclothes. Out of his haversack he pulled a set of fine breeches and yanked them on, followed by a shirt and a shawl-collared vest. He tied a brown cravat around his neck, slipped on good shoes and then donned a frock coat. He stuffed his mask under his old clothes in the haversack and left the bag in the shadows.

Using bricks and the drainpipe for support, Modo climbed down the wall. After ensuring his clothes were on straight, he stepped nonchalantly to the front door, took a good, deep breath and knocked.

CHAPTER 8

The Young Londoners Exploratory Society

M odo smoothed a few more creases from the front of his coat and wondered if the men he was about to meet would notice that it wasn't as finely stitched as theirs. He hoped the lights would be dim. He would have worn a top hat, but he had yet to find an affordable one. A collapsible, spring-loaded hat like the ones gentlemen wore to the opera would be perfect. He could slip it into his haversack and pop it open whenever he needed it. He knocked again.

The door opened an inch to reveal a single red-veined eye. "What do you want?" a gruff voice said.

"I'm here to attend the meeting. I do apologize for being tardy, sir. My driver had great difficulty finding the address. In fact, I was in such a hurry I left my hat in my carriage."

The eye didn't blink. "And your name is?"

"Robert Peterkin," Modo said without hesitation. "I'm an associate of Mr. Oscar Featherstone. I'm sorry, am I at the correct address? This is 22 Balcombe Street, is it not?"

"That is the address." The eye still hadn't blinked.

"I apologize if I'm not following the usual protocol. Yesterday I met Mr. Featherstone at the Crystal Palace. I'm an acquaintance of his sister." At the mention of Audrette, the man raised his eyebrow. "We attend the same painting courses. She's a very fine painter. In any case, I had a most pleasant discussion with Mr. Featherstone and I expressed my interest in scientific discovery and the exploration of . . ." Modo wished he'd asked Audrette what exactly the society explored. ". . . the sciences. Mr. Featherstone mentioned your society and invited me to attend a meeting. Have I come at a bad time?"

"No." The eye finally blinked and the door opened into a gloomy foyer.

Modo hoped he was properly put together. His hair! He'd completely forgotten his hair! Had he grown it to an appropriate length? He put his hand to his head and was relieved to find a thick mop. He patted it into place as he stepped into the house and watched the man lock the door behind him. The man had dark hair and mutton chops and intense steady eyes.

"Please forgive me, Mr. Peterkin, I haven't introduced myself. I'm Edwin Fuhr, head of the Young Londoners Exploratory Society; we are an official branch of the Society of Science. As it turns out, you aren't late for the meeting. We have been delayed. Please follow me."

Modo fell in behind Fuhr. Even in his transformed state he was dwarfed by the man, who led Modo down a hallway. Fuhr's gait was jerky, as though transporting his bulk was difficult. Modo heard an odd hissing sound but couldn't identify its source.

They passed three pairs of India rubber boots. One pair was grey with mud and the smell of sewage emanated from it. Modo breathed through his mouth. He noticed that Fuhr's trousers were splashed with brown matter around the knees. It hadn't rained in a few days. Perhaps he had been mucking about in the garden. Though, Modo couldn't picture this particular man clipping vines and pulling weeds.

"We are gathering in here," Fuhr said, opening a door and directing Modo inside a small library where three young gentlemen sat on a bench, talking animatedly.

At the sight of Modo they paused, looked him over with some curiosity, then resumed their conversation. Behind them, standing motionless, was a man almost as large as Fuhr. In the shadows at his feet sat a big, keen-eyed foxhound with an unnaturally bulky head. Its eyes followed Modo.

None of these people was Oscar Featherstone. Had he made a mistake?

"Mr. Featherstone is in the atrium," Fuhr said, as though reading Modo's mind. "We shall join him shortly. He is setting up a telescope." He raised his hand to signal the other hulking man to open the door into the atrium.

Once again Modo noted the jerky motion of Fuhr's arm, followed by a slight hiss. The sound was coming from Fuhr himself!

Everyone filed into the atrium, blocking his view of the room. Modo was about to follow them, but Fuhr put a hand on his shoulder. It tightened like a vise. "Not yet, Mr. Peterkrone."

"It's Peterkin," Modo replied, trying unsuccessfully to extricate himself from Fuhr's hand.

"My apologies, young sir. Peter*kin*. Yes. I need you to fill out some declaration forms, please. The discoveries of the Society are not for public consumption. At least, not yet." He released Modo and patted his back with a hand solid as iron.

"Forms? Yes, of course. I'll gladly fill them out."

"They're in here." Fuhr guided Modo to a candlelit table in the corner of a small, windowless room. "Read them very carefully, then sign."

"Yes, sir."

The table was littered with papers and various maps. One map was of London; several areas had been circled. Modo heard a *click* on the other side of the room, but at that moment a paper stamped with a symbol of a clock face in a triangle caught his eye. On the same page was a schematic that looked like a drawing of a machine with legs, of all things. With the expertise of a magician he rolled it up with one hand and tucked it into his sleeve. Under the drawing was another set of papers labelled: *Minutes of the Young Londoners Exploratory Society.* He skimmed it:

Citizen Fuhr in the chair.
Members present: Citizens Boon, Saxe-Coburg,

Cournet, Eccarius, Featherstone, Hales, Glyn,
and Yarrow.
  The Minutes of the preceding meeting having
been read and confirmed . . .

Saxe-Coburg—that name he'd read in the paper. It had something to do with the Royals, but he couldn't remember what.

He was about to roll up the minutes when Modo recalled a lesson Tharpa had drilled into him. Never turn your back to your enemy. Such a simple rule and he had already forgotten it.

"I'm sorry, sir, but there don't seem to be any forms," Modo said, turning to catch Fuhr locking the door to the library. Modo guessed the click he'd heard had been the other door being locked too, and he cursed himself for being so stupid.

"You won't need to sign any forms, Peterkin," Fuhr said. "This is not an organization you can be invited to join. Every member is chosen by me."

"Chosen," Modo repeated. "Oh, I see. I have unwittingly overstepped the boundaries of propriety. I deeply regret my error." Though he'd kept his tone calm, his eyes darted left and right, looking for a way out.

Fuhr glared at him openly. "Who sent you?" There was another hiss and his shoulders shifted and enlarged slightly.

Modo couldn't make sense of what he was seeing.

"No one. As I told you, I met Mr. Featherstone at—"

"At the Crystal Palace. I remember. But Mr. Featherstone was with me all day yesterday. So your supposed meeting could not have happened."

"Oh, I remember now." Modo banged the heel of his hand on his forehead. "It was actually two days ago. With his sister."

"Rubbish!" Fuhr bellowed, and Modo shuddered. "Mr. Featherstone is an only child."

"Only child? But I . . ." Was the man lying? He had to be. Audrette was real; she had come to his door, had been only inches from him. Or had Modo misunderstood her? Was she a cousin? No. Sister. She'd said sister. Maybe she'd lied about their relationship and was romantically linked with Featherstone. *But why would she mislead me?*

Fuhr tightened his fists and lumbered closer. "Who sent you? Tell me, boy." His shoulders continued to swell, pressing against the fabric of his jacket. A metallic clinking could be heard from under the garment.

"No one sent me. I—"

"Liar!" Fuhr's face twisted with anger.

Modo thought he saw mist rising from Fuhr's collar and then from the buttonholes of his suit coat. The hissing grew louder. Modo stepped back, bumping the table.

Steam! It was steam!

Fuhr grabbed Modo's collar. "You will tell me who sent you, boy, if I have to break every bone in your body."

"But, sir, sir, have mercy," Modo cried out. "Have mercy!"

"No one will hear you. They are gone. Now, answer my question."

"Uh, yes . . ." Modo flailed about until his hand hit a coat rack. Tharpa's voice came to him: *Anything can be a weapon.* The thick wooden pole would be hard enough to brain someone. Modo grabbed it and swung at Fuhr's temple, but Fuhr lifted his forearm and the pole broke into two over it. Fuhr punched Modo in the chest and Modo grunted; it felt like his ribs had caved in.

Steam geysered out of the seams of the giant's clothing. He swung his massive arm again and Modo caught hold of it, so Fuhr slammed him up against the wall. Modo wrenched himself away, ripping the sleeve from Fuhr's jacket. Modo's jaw dropped. The man's arm was made of metal! Pistons pushed back and forth between steel bones, the steam pumping out of holes in narrow iron plates. When Fuhr swung again, Modo ducked and the man's fist pounded a hole in the wall. Modo shuddered to think what such a blow would do to his skull.

Then Fuhr grabbed Modo by the neck, the metallic fingers closing around his windpipe.

"No. Stop!" Modo gasped, looking for some way to distract the man. Fuhr squeezed tighter until Modo could no longer breathe.

"You should not have interfered in our affairs," Fuhr said.

In a last desperate act, Modo jammed his feet against the wall and lunged forward with all his strength, breaking free of Fuhr's grip. Gagging and coughing, he found himself in the centre of the room. He stumbled, then ran and threw himself at the nearest door, hoping and praying his strength and speed would be enough to break it down.

He hit it hard with his shoulder and, accidentally, his head. He heard a *crack*, but the door didn't budge. Modo crumpled to the floor as darkness blotted out all thought.

CHAPTER 9

The Singing Sparrow

Oppie delivered a meal of pork buttons and mashed potatoes to Mr. W's room. He knocked and waited, knocked again, but there was no answer. He wolfed down a few pieces of pork, then lowered the plate to the floor. It would be safe enough here: the lame dog couldn't climb the stairs and Oppie hadn't yet seen a rat in these halls.

It was unusual for Mr. W to be away at mealtime. He seemed to carry on with his business only at night; that is, Oppie had never seen him go out during the day. The chamber pot would be set outside the door every evening, its collection another of Oppie's duties. Unlike most tenants, Mr. W would leave at least a few pence next to the pot.

Besides the extra money, Mr. W had given Oppie much advice through the closed door. He'd told the boy he was wise for his age and that his interest in reading should be pursued so he could rise to a better station. He'd also said, "You could be a detective too, young Oppie. You remind me of me when I was younger. You've got sharp eyes and a quick mind."

Oppie liked that. *A quick mind.*

Mr. W had promised to read him a little more of *Varney the Vampire*. Oppie shuddered at the possibility that such a bloodsucking creature might exist. He peered over his shoulder. *You're all in a twitter*, he told himself. He tromped down the stairs, though, hoping the noise would ward away anything that might be lurking in the darkness.

"Go on home, lad," the innkeeper muttered when Oppie stomped into the pub. "You're done for today."

Oppie left and trudged along the sidewalk in the dark. His mother was likely still over a ways on Exeter Street, clutching a worn basket and shouting, "Apple a pence!" If he hurried he'd catch her and they could walk home together.

He scratched at the lice on his scalp, then patted his pocket to be sure his coin purse hadn't gone missing. Fourpence for a whole day of work at the inn, plus the twopence the beautiful woman had given him. His mother had likely earned the same amount. His father would have made nothing because some sickness had crawled down his throat and now he was trapped in his bed at home, yellow and thin and moaning about being "just anofer moot ta feed."

Oppie was taking a shortcut down an alley when he remembered his friends saying they'd heard a child had disappeared in this very same alley a week ago. Was it Varney the Vampire who took him? The boy had been younger than Oppie so he probably had short, slow legs. *I can outrun anyone*, thought Oppie. Besides, the alley was a quicker way to Exeter Street. He shooed a cat out of his path and ran on.

When he heard the chirping of a bird, he slowed down. Its music was out of place in the grey light amid the shuttered windows of the buildings. Hundreds of chamber pots had been dumped into the gutter. The smell made his eyes water.

He spotted a flash of silver on a broken, rusted oil lamp. Moving closer he discovered a metallic sparrow perched on the lip of the lamp. It was a clockwork toy, chittering away. It had to be worth a fortune! If he could sell it his family would live off the money for a month. Who had left it here for any quick-fingered sort to snatch? Maybe the bobbies had set up the bird as a trap. He looked around furtively and, deciding he was safe, reached for the sparrow, grasping only air as the bird hopped away. He lunged at it again and it fluttered to a pipe sticking out of some stonework.

"I'll be," Oppie whispered, licking his lips. The creature's lifelike eyes rolled back and forth, taunting him. "You must be dreaming, Oppie." He narrowed one eye as though sighting a gun and jumped, his hands grabbing for the bird frantically.

This time the sparrow flapped high into the air, twirled around twice and landed two yards away. It pecked in a circle as though hunting for seeds, then disappeared around a turn in the alley.

Oppie raced ahead to discover the bird sitting on a banged-up crate. It was rubbing at its beak with one wing. It looked at Oppie and cheeped insistently. What wondrous clockwork made it tick? As he edged closer, it flitted up to his eye level and began flying down the alley. Oppie broke into a run, only a step or two behind the glittering bird, once even brushing its metal tail feathers with his fingertips. When it flapped through a doorway, he followed without a thought.

The bird landed on a man's outstretched hand. Oppie looked up at him. The man was dressed like a gentleman, with top hat and all, but his hair was long and as white as St. Nick's. His skin was pale.

"Do you like my pet?" he asked.

"Yes! It's a true wonder. I wasn't going to take it, honest!"

"I believe you." The old man placed a seed on his palm and the bird pecked at it. "I'm Dr. Cornelius Hyde and I am so pleased to meet a young specimen such as yourself."

"Pleased to meet you too, guvnuh."

The man reached into his greatcoat pocket and produced a second sparrow, which he cupped in his other hand. It chirped. "Would you like a bird of your own?"

Oppie nodded.

"Then come with me."

Oppie paused. His mother wouldn't want him to follow a stranger. But a bird of his own! Maybe two! He could play with them and later they would fetch a good price. Mum would rub his head and hug him and say, "You're a good un', darlin'."

The man set a bird on either shoulder, opened a door and proceeded down a hallway, while the sparrows sang, their lively marble eyes mesmerizing Oppie, who hurried to keep up.

CHAPTER 10

A Friendly Interrogation

"Hrrts."

The raspy voice echoed in the near dark. Modo couldn't tell where it was coming from.

"*Hrrdrs id . . .*"

His throat was parched and his head throbbed. Shadows passed in front of him, but his eyes felt too sore to keep open. He shut them tight.

"*Monnm. Mere mere. Id hrrds. Missshus Feeenchley, help. I hurt.*"

So. It was his own voice. He tried to touch his lips but couldn't move his hands.

"You are in much torment," a woman said flatly. She had an odd accent. "Do you want your mother?"

Modo opened his eyes in anger, only to be blinded by a bright light. "I—I have no mother."

"That is rather sad."

Her face came into focus. It was perfect and pale, like the Greek goddesses he'd seen in the paintings Mrs. Finchley had shown him. She had determined blue eyes and tightly braided red hair. She straightened up and stepped back a few feet.

"You gave yourself a severe blow."

At once Modo remembered fleeing Fuhr and striking the door. He couldn't recall anything after that. He tried again to lift his arms, then realized his wrists and ankles were manacled to the thick wooden chair upon which he was slumped.

"Count your lucky stars that you're still amongst the living," the woman said, studying him.

With a start he wondered if his transformation had lasted. He'd never been knocked out while in this state. Blood pounded in his ears. He tried to touch his face but only rattled the manacles. His eyes searched the woman's expression for any hint of disgust or revulsion, and finding none, he concluded that he had maintained his form.

"You are too curious, young man," she said. "Curiosity can lead to fatality." She chuckled as though she'd been terribly clever.

He could now make out the gas light, magnified by tin reflectors, directed at his face. He couldn't see anyone else in the room.

"Wh-wh-where am I?" he asked.

"I will ask questions, you will answer," she explained. "I am Miss Hakkandottir. Now you know my name, tell me yours."

"It's Mo—Mr. Peterkin. Robert Peterkin. What do you want with me?"

There was a flash of metal, then pain raked his right cheek. He screamed and strained against his manacles.

"I ask questions, you answer. It is a simple arrangement. Do you understand?"

Modo nodded, blood dripping down his face. Red stains spattered across his white sleeve.

"Now, Mr. Peterkin. Under other circumstances, I would be patient, perhaps even hospitable, but there is no time. You have infiltrated our organization, so I need to know: who employs you?"

He couldn't tell them about Miss Featherstone. Chances were that she knew little if anything about the true nature of this Society and he was certain they would do her harm.

He ran his sandpaper tongue around the inside of his mouth. His forehead was sweating. "An uncle," he said, "of one of your members. Of . . ." He struggled to remember the names on the list. Mr. Socrates had made him work hard on his memorization skills, but he was failing nonetheless. "Saxe-Romburg," he said.

"Saxe-Coburg," the woman corrected. She tilted her head inquisitively, a flattering angle that made her more beautiful. Except for her eyes; they were reptilian. She rarely blinked, which Modo found most disconcerting. "But you originally inquired about Mr. Featherstone. Are you lying to me?"

Modo shook his head quickly, twitching in anticipation of another blow. "No. No. I was simply trying to throw you off the track of my employer, that was all."

"How did you know Mr. Featherstone was a member of our Society?"

"Mr. Saxe-Coburg is a friend of his, or so I assumed."

Her eyes burned into his. "So the Royals hired you?"

"Yes, an uncle. Renald. He's overprotective, by his own admission."

"Renald. The name isn't familiar to me. And I know all of them."

"He lives in Bonn."

She tapped her temple with her finger, and Modo shook his head and looked again. Could it be? It seemed her hand was made of metal, each digit cut in such a way that her fingers curled and moved in the same manner as flesh and bone. She looked at her finger. With a *schlickt* a razor-sharp nail suddenly appeared. It looked long enough to cut his throat. "You are not telling the truth."

She stepped closer. Modo tried to edge away, straining so hard to break the manacles that he felt a vein pop out on his forehead. The claw marks in his cheek burned.

Her metal hand gently brushed his cheek, spiderlike. The tips of her fingernails were cold. Fine piano wires extended from her wrist up into the flesh of her arm.

"It is unwise to lie to me," she said softly. She pointed her index finger at his left eye, and Modo pressed himself against the back of the chair, trying to avoid it. "I must know why you are interested in Saxe-Coburg. Who sent you?"

"I—I don't know," he whimpered. "I only accept investigations through the post. I—I never meet my clients in person."

Her finger was less than an inch away and he couldn't tell if her nail was still extended. Now she pressed her finger against his eyeball.

Modo let out an anguished grunt. "Stop! Don't! No!" He spat the words. Would his eye break open? He thought of an egg leaking yolk. "Please! Please! I'll tell you anything."

"How do you communicate with these clients of yours?"

"As I said, by letter."

"When do you next expect them to contact you?" With each word she increased the pressure on his eye.

"Ahhh! Tomorrow. Tomorrow! A letter will be waiting for me."

"Where?"

"The . . . the Red Horn. Room—*ahhh*—three." He was surprised how well he could lie, even with pain clouding his mind. "Please, don't. My eye. My eye!"

"It is a beautiful eye," she said. "It would be a shame to have to blind it."

She withdrew her finger. Modo pulled in a breath like a bellows, filling his lungs as though he hadn't breathed in weeks. His vision blurred; he couldn't stop the tears. He wanted to weep, to lash out at his tormentor.

"What have you learned?" she asked.

He blinked and blinked until he could see more clearly.

"That I should go back to my country cottage and give up detective work."

She laughed. "Humour. Even at such a dire time. How courageous. What I meant was, what have you learned about *us*?"

"Only that you are a scientific organization. That's all. I was just beginning my investigation. My employer asked me to follow and take notes about the group's activities."

He blinked away a few more tears, closed his left eye and used his good one. She looked concerned and, curiously, a little frightened.

"Are you unwell?" she asked.

He wanted to shout, *Of course, you witch! You nearly poked my eye out!* Instead he said, "I don't understand."

"You have blotches on your skin and your face seems to be swelling."

Modo felt his bones beginning to shift slowly, his muscles starting to sag. He couldn't control them any longer. It had always worked this way. After a few hours his muscles refused to hold their shape. This time the torment and exhaustion had sped up the process.

He coughed up phlegm, and seeing her alarmed reaction, he did it again, only louder. Then, for effect, he gagged on his saliva, letting his tongue loll out.

"You *are* ill," she said, taking a step back. She pulled a handkerchief from her vest pocket and wiped off her hand. "What have you got?"

"It's nothing," Modo whispered. "Just a cough. I've been under the weather for the past few days. It's not consumption, if that's what you're thinking."

Her once perfectly serene face looked very uncomfortable. Modo spat out a mouthful of slime, and she jumped back. He nearly grinned; he had an advantage now. That's how Mr. Socrates had trained him: *Find your opponent's weakness and exploit it.* Modo coughed again.

Hakkandottir backed up all the way to the door and knocked on it with her metal hand.

The door opened and in walked Fuhr, his joints hissing. The foxhound padded behind him. Intelligence and anger glared from its eyes and its skull reflected light. Modo blinked three times before he could see clearly that it had been moulded from metal. How could that be?

Fuhr's cold eyes cut across Modo, then settled on Hakkandottir. "He's alive."

"Yes, so far. His knowledge of our operation appears limited."

"I could interrogate him, if you like."

Modo's stomach churned.

Hakkandottir shook her head. "No. He is a small cog. His interest in Featherstone and, especially, Saxe-Coburg is distressing. Peterkin may not know much, but I suspect his masters do. We must move faster. Is the transportation complete?"

"Yes. The subjects have had the laudanum and have been moved to the lower station."

"Then we are finished here. They will soon receive their final dose."

Fuhr's arm hissed as he pointed at Modo. "What about him?"

Hakkandottir shrugged. "He is of no value now and neither is this house." With a flick of her metal hand, she knocked the oil lamp off the desk, and fire exploded across the floor. Fuhr, the hound, and Hakkandottir walked through the door and closed it without a backward glance.

Tongues of flame danced around Modo, the polished hardwood perfect kindling. He struggled and kicked, trying to break free of the wooden chair. Tharpa hadn't taught him what to do in this situation.

CHAPTER 11

Wolf Sick

That same evening a letter arrived at the Langham Hotel and was slid under the door of room 443. Octavia Milkweed frowned, set her ragged copy of *Frankenstein* on the reading table, and retrieved the missive. She read it, committed its contents to memory, then lit it with the candle and let it burn in the brass sink. She turned on the taps and washed the ashes down the drain.

After scrubbing the rouge from her cheeks, she changed into shabby grey clothes and tucked her hair under a plain bonnet. If she were to be seen in the hotel dressed in this fashion, a porter would toss her into the gutter. She pushed aside the thick curtains, opened the window, looked around and stepped out onto the small faux balcony. Her fourth-floor room wasn't a wise choice for this part of her employment, but at least it faced Bond Street, which wasn't half as busy as Regent, especially now that most of the clerks had gone home. She climbed down easily and dropped to the ground.

As she walked along Bond Street she examined the letter in her mind's eye. It was all quite straightforward. She imagined similar letters being sent to agents throughout the city— throughout England, in fact, and other parts of the world, each cog assigned its task. It was boggling to think of the size of the organization. Or perhaps she was the only agent out on this particular night.

No, that at least wasn't true. She guessed that Mr. Wellington, unwittingly, was doing their bidding as well. Her thoughts had turned to him several times during the course of the day. His voice had sounded youthful. She had only ever met two other agents and they had been pudgy old spiders.

Mr. Wellington had spoken in lower tones and there was a softness in his voice that had touched her. And, he didn't sound bitter.

She wondered what he looked like. She pictured him with mutton chops and laughed. No, that's what sailors and old men wore. But maybe well-trimmed hair with a bit of a curl and a straight, narrow nose.

When Octavia was a child in the orphanage, she had often dreamed a man would come to rescue her. He would say, "I'm your father and my ship was wrecked—that is why you are here in the orphanage. Now I can take you home." Or he would be a rich uncle. As she grew older, she hoped it would be a young prince and she pictured him so frequently she could actually see his face. In the end no one came, so one day she left on her own and began her life as a pickpocket.

She couldn't help imagining Mr. W as the young prince she'd dreamed about as a child. *You're being a bufflehead, Octavia.* She laughed. Mr. Wellington might well be as ugly as Old Taff, who had taught her to survive on the streets. Besides, there had been one prince in her life already, Garret, Taff's "adopted" son. He was the closest she'd had to a big brother. But thinking of him saddened her, so she let the image of his dark hair and eyes fade.

She approached the Breckham Moral and Industrial School, an old jailhouse that had been converted into an orphanage and training school. The sight of it reminded her of Lady Cotterel's Orphanage, where they had attempted to shape her, one smack of the rod at a time. She'd hated them, they'd hated her.

But never mind. She was now dressed as a charwoman, in the employ of an imaginary lady. And this was not Lady Cotterel's; this school was doing good work, training young abandoned girls and sending them to Canada or Australia to work.

She banged the knocker and the clang echoed in the night. Soft footsteps approached the other side of the door. It opened and a young girl in a black dress squinted at her.

"What ye be 'ere for?" she muttered, and, before Octavia could answer, a broom appeared from behind the door and swatted the girl across the head.

From the shadows of the hall a ragged, tired voice admonished her. "You say 'Good evening' when you open the door after six o'clock. That is the proper greeting. How many times must I repeat it?" A hand pinched the ear of the cowering girl and yanked her away from the door. "Get to your bed!"

The orphan ran off down the hall, holding her ear and sobbing. An old woman in a brown dress stepped out of the shadows. "Good evening. How may I be of assistance?" The stink of boiled cabbage emanated from the house—or from the woman. It was a smell Octavia hated. Cabbage was all they had served for breakfast, lunch and dinner at Lady Cotterel's.

"Are you the governess?"

"Yes. It is half past nine bells. Most of the house is in bed."

"I am here to inquire about a prospect for Lady Mordray. I did not question my Lady's orders."

"Ah, well, you are a good, obedient sort then . . ." she said, turning her head so her voice carried down the hall, "unlike *some* in this house."

The woman reminded Octavia a little of Lady Cotterel. A few short years ago Octavia had been very much like the girl who had answered the door. For a moment her heart ached.

"So which prospect are you inquiring about?"

"My Lady says she wants to know about Ester McGravin."

The woman lifted one eyebrow, then licked her lips, exposing a set of wooden false teeth.

"Ester has taken ill."

"Ill? My Lady will not be pleased to hear that. She needs a replacement immediately."

"I have other prospects, much further along in their training."

"My Lady insisted on Ester McGravin. What illness does the child have?"

"A fever. She will no doubt be healthy in a few days. Next time you inquire please come during the day; it would be more convenient."

Octavia nodded. "I will report to Lady Mordray and return when she sends me."

The old governess closed the door with a *thud*, and Octavia walked back to the street, mulling over her orders. The letter had stated clearly that she must immediately see this Ester McGravin face to face and note her condition, including, of all things, the appearance of her shoulders. The only details about Ester that Octavia had been given were that her hair was red and she was ten years old.

Octavia walked to the end of the block and looked around to be sure no one was watching. She turned a corner and found an alley that led to the back of the school. She hid behind a bush. Normally, Octavia would observe a house for days before breaking into it, getting to know the patterns of the people who lived there. Old Taff had taught her that. But she didn't have days.

Only one light burned in the building, near the front, so she chose a main-floor window at the back. She crept to it and pulled hard on its frame. It opened to one side with a squeak. She poked her head inside and listened. She heard someone snoring, then a few deep breaths and more snoring. The dull moonlight glinted off a metal bed. Octavia climbed quietly onto the sill, and then slowly lowered her feet to the floor, waiting for her eyes to adjust. Soon she could make out three beds containing three girls each, packed in together like sausages. No need to buy another bed if you can fit them all in one. She remembered those days far too well. One girl snored loudly. Octavia was thankful for that. It would help cover up any noise she made. She crept across the complaining hardwood to the door and opened it, peering into the hall.

"What's you want 'ere?" a tiny voice asked from inside the room.

Octavia froze.

"Miss. Miss. What's you want 'ere?" The girl who had answered the door to Octavia sat up in bed, rubbing her eyes.

"I'm doing an inspection," Octavia whispered, crossing the floor back to the girl's bedside. "Go to sleep."

"Can't sleep. Ear 'urts. What you inspectin' for?"

"I've come to see Ester McGravin."

The girl frowned. "Ester? Why?"

"She's me mate." Octavia slipped easily into her former dialect.

The girl blinked. "Your mate? And you want 'er out of 'ere before she's shipped to 'stralia or worse?"

"Rather! Do you know where they've stowed 'er?"

"Ester is wolf sick." The girl said this as though it completely answered the question.

"Wolf sick?"

"Yes. She howls 'n' barks. She went out to get eggs, was gone a fortnight. When she comes back she's all hairy. She's wolf sick."

"I see. I'd still like to know where me mate is. We've been friends for a long time."

"In the cellar where the bad girls go."

"How do I get there?"

"I'll show you."

The girl brushed past Octavia and tiptoed down the hall-way. Octavia checked both ways, then followed her. They took one turn, then another and finally the girl stopped at a wood-slat door that came to a point at the top.

"I ent going down there with you."

Octavia leaned over and gave her a kiss on the forehead.

"Wot's that for?"

"Thank you. You should go get your forty winks now."

But the girl stayed and watched as Octavia heaved open the large door and felt her way down the stairs. The room was dank and clouded with a smell so sour it forced her to pinch her nose. Perhaps it had been a cesspool before the sewers were built under London.

In a corner on the far side of the room, a blue, ghostly light shone from behind a black curtain. Between her and the curtain, she could make out broken chairs, old clothing, a pile of coal and pots and pans. The floor of the cellar was earthy and damp. She would slip if she wasn't careful. She picked her way gingerly over a pile of bricks and through other rubbish until she reached the curtain. She pulled it back and gasped.

There, on a thick oak table, chained by her legs and arms, was a young girl with red hair. *Ester.* The oil lamp hanging from the ceiling threw so many shadows that at first glance she looked like a normal child, but as Octavia's eyes focused in the dimness, she realized that Ester's face was unnaturally elongated, her nose flat and wide, and clumps of her hair had fallen out and lay around her on the table. Her muscular arms and legs were covered with reddish fuzz. She wore leggings that were in tatters, as though she'd crawled over sharp stones, and her dirty feet were malformed.

Wolf sick. Now she understood what the little girl had meant! Octavia committed every detail to memory, just as the letter had instructed, and carefully inspected Ester's shoulders. Sure enough, there was something odd about them. She inched closer. One large, shiny iron bolt stuck out of the top of each shoulder, piercing the girl's clothing and reaching almost the height of her ears. Octavia pulled at the slits in Ester's dress to reveal fresh stitches etched on either side of the bolts.

Octavia's stomach began to heave. She'd seen many gruesome sights in her short life, but after seeing this she took longer than usual to compose herself.

Who would do this to a little girl? The governess? Was she conducting some sort of horrible experiment? If she was, then she had important friends, for this required a surgeon. Octavia had heard rumours of street urchins disappearing. Perhaps the governess was somehow involved. Or she had found Ester in this wolf-sick state and didn't want to lose her investment, so she chained her down here hoping the sickness would run its course and Ester could return to her normal life in the orphanage. But what on earth were the shoulder bolts for?

Ester lay still as death. Octavia slowly reached out and touched a bolt. The metal was cold. Ester moaned, a low ululation. Octavia noticed marks on her legs and arms from the shackles, scabs and weeping sores. She'd been lying here a few days. Octavia considered trying to wake the girl, but all the letter had asked for was her observations.

Just as she took a step to leave, the girl's eyes popped
open. She glanced frantically around until she saw Octavia.

"Huh-huh-hoo ur you?" she rasped.

"I'm a . . . a mate."

"Arms hurt. Free me."

The orders had said to observe her. Nothing else. *Well, I
can observe her as she goes to the doctor*, she thought. The
hospital for children wasn't that far away and she had enough
money for a cab. That wouldn't really be disobeying orders.

"Me hurt. Me do," Ester whispered. "Must go back to
Orlando."

"Orlando? Where is that?"

"Home. Safe. Drink."

She was mad as a hatter! The doctors would figure it
out. On a hunch, Octavia searched several cluttered tables,
pushing aside nails, a broken doll and clay pieces, until
she found a key. She plunged it into the lock on the left
ankle manacle and it turned. Ester moved her leg ever so
slightly. It took Octavia a minute to release the remaining manacles. Ester rolled over and moaned. It would be
near impossible to carry her out, given her weakened state.
She'd be dead weight.

"I'll help you," Octavia said, feeling she had no choice
but to try. "There's a hospital nearby. Put your arm over
my shoulder."

With unexpected strength and speed, the girl planted
both feet on the ground and shoved Octavia back. She fell
to the floor.

"No touch me! So says the voice."

Octavia rubbed her head as she climbed to her feet, surprised to find herself halfway across the room. She moved
to grab hold of Ester, but before she could do so Ester head-
butted her in the rib cage and Octavia fell to the floor again.

Footsteps pounded upstairs, followed by a yell. The governess must have been alerted!

Ester shook her head, squeezing her temples. "The
voices! Must go back to Orlando." Then she was charging
up the stairs.

A child screamed, and Octavia remembered the little girl
she'd left on the landing. She took the stairs three at a time
and found her in a trembling heap on the floor, surrounded
by shattered glass. The window above her was broken, curtains flapping in the breeze.

"Don't move!" Octavia insisted. "You'll cut your feet."

"What's going on?" The silhouette of the governess
appeared at the far end of the hall.

Octavia patted the girl's head, then followed Ester out
the broken window.

CHAPTER 12

Fire!

Modo coughed and tried to gulp air, but all he inhaled was smoke. His heart thudded. His body was slipping back into its natural shape. As he changed his wrists grew meatier, pressing against the manacles. He yanked his arm away from the chair, hoping to snap the metal or break the armrest, but he'd grown too weak.

He thought of Mrs. Finchley. If only she'd come and save him! He wished Tharpa were here too. Now. Tharpa would break the manacles and carry Modo to freedom.

I'm going to die! he thought. They would never know what had happened to him. Once he'd allowed the thought to enter his head it kept repeating: *I'll die, I'll die, die, die.*

He sucked in more smoke, coughing deeply. He *would* die if he kept thinking like that. He knew better! Tharpa had taught him how to wriggle out of ropes and how to pick locks, but both his hands were bound by manacles. His wrists had now mushroomed, so the restraints cut into his skin. Another thick cough shook his chest. The dark hair he'd grown was falling out in clumps, sizzling on the floor. Sweat trickled down his forehead. He was failing Mr. Socrates' test.

I'm sorry, Mr. Socrates! I'm sorry!

"You naughty brat."

Modo's heart leapt. "Mrs. Finchley?" he moaned into the smoke. "Mrs. Finchley!" No, she wasn't there. His brain was addled, but he remembered one of the times she'd called him a brat. She had left a jar of sweet biscuits on the highest bookshelf in his room, believing he couldn't reach it. But he climbed the door frame, grabbed the jar and landed softly on the floor. Triumphantly he lifted the lid, only to discover he couldn't fit his hand into the jar. In a moment of inspiration he'd transformed his hand into a smaller one, pushed it inside and grabbed a biscuit. Overjoyed, he lost control of his transformation and his hand snapped back to its bulbous shape, becoming stuck in the jar. That was how Mrs. Finchley found him. "Oh, Modo, you naughty brat," she had said, chuckling in that soft, sweet way. "You've got to get your own self out of this—I'm not breaking my best jar." Then she said, "You know, Modo, you could have turned it over and poured the biscuits out."

Another bout of coughing and gagging interrupted his reverie. No air. He fell forward, expecting to faint, and then he remembered: smoke rises. He lowered his head between his knees and took a few desperate breaths.

That's when it occurred to him: the biscuit jar! That was the answer. He was able to do it then; he could do it now. The transformation began in his imagination, just by picturing his hand smaller, thinner. He coughed so hard he thought he would spit blood. He forced himself to hold his breath, just to stop the coughing for a few moments. Again he concentrated on the transformation of his right hand.

His wrist grew smaller. His bones were now pressing tightly against one another. There was nowhere for his flesh to go. He needed air badly, but if he let himself breathe he would cough and then he would be done for. He pulled his hand back from the manacle as hard as he could.

"I won't die here!" He wanted to see Mrs. Finchley again, Mr. Socrates, Tharpa. And, Miss Featherstone.

That her face should come to him at this moment surprised him, but it gave him an extra surge of strength, and by allowing the manacle to tear away a piece of his skin, he was at last able to free his hand. In his pain he sucked in a lungful of smoke. Hacking and coughing, he grabbed his throat. The flames were so close they licked at his feet.

"No," he shouted, "you can't have me!"

He slammed his fist against the opposite arm of the chair until it cracked and the chain fell loose, dangling from his other hand.

He could see clearly only through his slightly larger eye; the other still ached too much from being poked by Miss Hakkandottir. Standing up, he lifted the chair so that the chains slipped off its legs. His feet were manacled together, but he could still take small, awkward steps. The heat was singeing his hair, and he had to slap out the sparks on his clothing.

With his last reserve of strength he staggered through the flames and, using his shoulder, smashed through the door and stumbled into the library, where he tripped over a stool and slid across the floor. Before him the bookshelves danced with flames. He saw a dim rectangular light to his left. The window! He picked up an ottoman and threw it through the window, then leapt over the frame, glass slicing open his smouldering clothes and leathery skin. Diving into the dewy grass, he rolled and shook himself until he was certain the flames were out.

Air. Pure, fresh air. He gasped and spluttered, spat ashes and took in another breath and another. Beside him, the house was alive with fire.

He lay there heaving, then wiped his face with his sleeve, noting that it was alight. Frantically he swatted it out.

"Fire! Fire!" a man yelled. "The Munsen house is burning. Alert the fire brigade!"

Soon Modo heard a chorus of voices and pounding footsteps.

"There's someone lying over there!"

Modo could not find the strength to get up, could only lie gasping as Londoners came rushing to see the spectacle. Soon a small crowd had gathered, including a few children; most of the spectators were in their nightclothes.

"He's hurt!" said a gentleman in a robe, his nightcap pulled down to his ears. "Can we help you, sir?"

Modo rolled away from them, keeping his face hidden behind his arm. "Yesss . . ." But the act of speaking made him cough and he accidentally moved his arm.

A young woman pointed at him. "Look at his face! It's . . . it's melted!"

The horror of her expression was more than he could stand. Modo looked away.

"Oh, how terrible," someone said.

He had to flee from them. Groaning, Modo sat up, his chains rattling madly. His features were clearly lit by the flames. Everyone backed away from him. The children hid behind their parents.

"Don't come any closer!" he shouted as a woman fainted. He covered his face with his hands. "Get away! Please go away!" He shook his arm again, clanging the chains.

"He's an escaped convict," a man shouted. "He must have started the fire!"

Modo stood shakily, then scrambled to the street, lurching into the dark.

The journey home, at first climbing from rooftop to rooftop, dragging the chains, nearly broke him. Even crawling was more than his body could bear. He finally gave up and lowered himself to the street. When a wagon carrying straw and manure and heading in the direction of Seven Dials stopped for a moment, he slipped into the back of it and crouched down, trying not to cough.

He struggled to climb the wall of the Red Boar, then pushed open the window to his room and tumbled to the floor. He stank of smoke and his throat was painfully dry. He grabbed the flask next to the bed and poured the last of its contents over his lips and across his face, wincing when the liquid hit his open wounds. His right hand, where the skin had been torn, was still bleeding. And his knuckles hadn't changed back to their original shape.

He stared at the ceiling. He needed rest, but his face was on fire from the scratches, his eyes stinging. He coughed up a mucus ball the size of a bat and spat it out on the floor.

"Mrs. Finchley . . . help," he whimpered. He longed for her soothing hands, her kind words. She had calmed him following the nightmares he'd had after the first time he saw himself in the mirror. He wished with all his heart that she would walk through his door and comfort him now. Maybe she would take him to Venice. She'd told him how many people wore masks in that city. He'd fit in perfectly. No one would try to kill him there.

He rubbed at his face, reached for his dirty sheets to wipe his eyes and nose. He looked at his hand in the moonlight. None of the wounds were deep enough for stitches. But they could go septic.

He pushed himself out of bed and lurched over to the dresser. He made a poultice from his few bottles of liniment and flour and pressed it against the cuts. That dulled the pain slightly. He glanced in the mirror to find that the cuts on his face weren't as deep as he had feared.

He picked the locks on the manacles using a pin and two nails, all the while cursing himself. He'd left behind his haversack and had ruined his only set of fancy clothes. They'd be expensive to replace.

Before opening his door he looked out the peephole to be sure no one was around. Waiting on the floor in the hall was a plate of pork buttons that looked as though they had been picked over by a cat. A glass of warm ale sat beside it, most likely a death trap for flies. He silently thanked little Oppie. These days the boy was the most dependable person in his life. Maybe he would one day invite him in and teach him to read a bit; that'd give the lad a leg up.

Modo took his dinner back to his bed and devoured the pork and drank the ale. One idea flared red in his mind: *I could have been burned alive! I was nearly murdered!* He shuddered. At least Hakkandottir would think he was dead and would not pursue him.

He had enough money to spend a day or two recovering, rather than working, but he wondered if he should warn Audrette Featherstone that her brother was part of a dangerous underground group. Then Modo remembered how Fuhr had insisted that Featherstone had no siblings.

If he was to be believed, who, then, was Audrette?

In his pocket he found the piece of paper on which she'd written the Featherstone address, examining it as though he might learn something from the handwriting. Had she known all along that this little assignment might result in his being killed?

He stumbled to his dresser, opened the top drawer and pensively examined his collection of masks. He picked up a black one, a night mask, his fingers tracing the nose and eyeholes, lost in thought. There was, after all, a mystery to be solved now. He put the mask on.

CHAPTER 13

The Hunter and the Hunted

Octavia ran down the streets, cursing her skirts and corset with every step. She'd always hated being restrained by women's clothing. Meanwhile Ester loped with feral speed and slyness. She darted here and there, leaping over fences and, finally, scrambling down the gaslit pathways in Regent's Park. Octavia followed, and once she reached the open grass she kicked off her shoes, snatched them up with one hand and lifted the hem of her dress with the other so she could run full tilt.

The gas lights were soon of little use because Ester slipped into the bushes off the path. Octavia chased her through a grove of trees, more bushes, past a statue. She was only five yards away. *I've got you now!*

She'd have to tie this girl up, but with what? The stays from her corset would be too difficult to get at. Her sash had her secret pouch—she couldn't lose that. Her hair ribbons! They would be long enough to tie several tight knots. She pulled off her bonnet, letting it drop to the ground, then felt around for the ribbons and yanked them out. Her long hair fell down her back.

But in that moment she'd lost sight of Ester. Octavia kept running straight, until ahead she saw a few branches move and heard a *thunk*. She burst through a line of bushes to discover a knoll, a fountain and another Greek statue, but no wolf-girl. She looked behind the statue. No sign of her, but there was a manhole lid set in the cobblestones. She'd heard stories of men who worked below London clearing the clogged sewers. Not a place she'd like to have tea, but it would be the perfect hidey-hole.

Octavia leaned over and grabbed hold of the cover's edge. She dug her feet into the ground, but was able to lift the lid only an inch, before dropping it with a *clang*. There was no way in heaven that Ester could have lifted it. Octavia found a thick branch, but it snapped the moment she tried to pry the lid off. Ester couldn't have hidden down there.

But then Octavia remembered the way Ester had thrown her—thrown her!—across the room. How her ribs still ached! This girl was unnaturally strong.

At last, perspiring, Octavia gave up on trying to lift the lid, and on capturing Ester. In any case, she had more than accomplished her assigned task. Ester was free of the orphanage, at least, though Octavia wasn't certain anymore that that was a good thing. However, if Ester *was* in the sewers she certainly seemed tough enough to face any danger she might find down there.

Octavia slipped her shoes on, took one last look around and walked out of the park. It was a few minutes before a cab passed down Hadford Street. She hailed it, and as the cabbie drove to the address she'd been given, she wrote her observations of Ester's condition using a pencil and a piece of paper she'd tucked into her sash. She bit her lip, concentrating; each bump made her hand jerk. She hoped the note would be legible. It was hard to tell in the dark.

She had the driver wait while she walked up the front path of the three-storey mansion, passing through a large iron gate. One corner of the house was a tall turret, its slit windows lit. The letter box at the front door was also in the shape of a turret. She dropped her letter into the draw-bridge of the letter box, and when the hinge closed, a soft bell sounded. She hurried to the carriage.

Back at the Langham, Octavia walked to the far side of the hotel and waited until Bond Street was clear. She checked to be sure no one was looking out the hotel windows, then hiked up her skirts and tucked them into her sash. She scaled the faux balconies to her room, and swung herself, legs first, into the open window. It wasn't exactly a graceful entrance; her dress caught on the iron latticework and she felt half-undressed by the time she'd squeezed in, kicking her way past the long heavy curtains. As she fought to tidy her skirts, she envied men their trousers. Her perfect life would be in a place where she could wear trousers all the time. On an island, perhaps. With a prince.

"Out for a stroll, were you?" a gruff voice snapped.

Octavia swallowed her panic and answered as calmly as she could. "I needed a bit of fresh air."

"Mmm. Is there no fresh air outside the front door?" The voice was coming from the far corner of the room.

"Sometimes a lady needs a little privacy." It was too dark to see anything. She had sown a small opening in her dress so that she could speedily slip her stiletto from a sheath worn around her left thigh. She grasped the handle. *I'll have one chance*, she told herself. *Strike hard.*

"Reaching for your weapon?" he asked.

She heard shuffling, a squeak of the floor. She caught her breath. "No, no. Only smoothing out my dress."

"Then remove your hand. Slowly."

She did, leaving the stiletto in its sheath. "I'm afraid you have me at a disadvantage, sir. I don't know your name."

"And I do not know yours, apparently. And therein lies the problem." He chuckled. "*Lies. The. Problem.* Yes, that is a very apt description of the situation. Lies. Lies. Lies."

She had no idea what he was going on about. He sounded as though he had a slate loose. Her eyes had adjusted and she could make out the lines of her bed, the dresser beside it and in the corner, on a chair, a lumpy shape.

She considered the distance: three or four yards at most. She could leap over and strike in a heartbeat. However, it was likely that he had a pistol.

"Why are you mumbling on about lies?" she asked.

"Because lies are what you are cloaked in."

"And how would you know that?" She took tiny imperceptible steps towards him, only to discover, to her horror, that there wasn't a man in the chair, just a coat dropped onto it. Her heart thudded.

"I want only the truth from you. What is your name?"

She was certain the voice was behind her now. She smelled smoke. "My name is none of your concern."

"Well, None of Your Concern, it is a pleasure to meet you. Again."

Again? His voice was indeed familiar, but it was so guttural and strained she couldn't recognize it.

He wheezed and grunted as though in distress. Octavia took some consolation in this; perhaps he was unwell, or even wounded. Maybe he had no intention to harm her. If he were an agent from Russia or Germany her throat would be slit by now. Unless, of course, he was planning to dispatch her *after* this strange interrogation.

"Are you unwell?" she asked, turning slowly towards his voice and looking for his shape in the dark.

"Oh, so now you're concerned for my health. How sweet, Miss Featherstone."

She felt a smile cross her lips.

"Mr. Wellington," she said to the curtains, "if, indeed, that is your real name. It is such a pleasure to meet you again."

CHAPTER 14

Revelations

"Stay where you are," Modo hissed from behind the velvet curtain. He could just make out her silhouette through a moth hole. He felt a stab of guilt for treating her this way, but the anger buzzing in his skull and the soreness in his hand and lungs reminded him why he'd dragged himself over rooftops to the Langham, wheezing the whole way. It had been her fault! She may not have been able to predict he would come so close to death, but chances were she knew he was being sent into danger.

"I don't trust you, Miss *Featherstone*. Not one iota."

"May I at least sit down? I've been rather busy myself this evening and a dainty lass such as I needs her rest."

Twice she had glanced in his direction. He was certain she knew where he was. He'd been able to throw his voice before to confuse her. Now there would be no point.

"Sit on the bed, then. But back away from the curtain."

"What will be the consequence if I don't?"

"I'm pointing a pistol at you. I shall shoot you straight through the heart."

"Ah, that's consequence enough. I prefer to keep my heart intact." She did as he instructed and sat on the edge of her bed just as he launched into a series of hacking coughs.

"Do you need syrup?" she asked. "I have some Daffy's Elixir, fresh from the apothecary."

"You'd likely poison me. And I've already been close enough to death tonight, thanks to you and your so-called brother. I thought the investigation into the nocturnal activities of Mr. Featherstone was to be a simple matter. I nearly died."

"I'm awfully sorry."

Was she being flippant? She didn't seem to be surprised by this or to have so much as a thimbleful of remorse.

"So, Mr. Wellington, how did you uncover my secret life?"

"I . . . When I accepted your case, I was . . . let us say, trusting. If I hadn't been so blinded by your . . ." He paused, remembering the way she'd dabbed at her lovely eyes with her handkerchief when she'd relayed the story of her brother. She had used her voice, beauty and charm to great effect. ". . . lies. I have since discovered that Oscar Featherstone has no sister."

"And how did you discover where I live?"

"I analyzed your handwriting."

"My handwriting told you where to go?"

"No. But you used a pen with a nearly dry inkwell. You had to retrace your writing several times. Hotels are notorious for being cheap with their inkwells."

"And how did you conclude I was staying at the Langham?"

"The watermark on the notepaper was an L. And do you remember the handkerchief you used to wipe your eyes?"

"Yes."

"It was embossed with an *L*. If you were not Mr. Feath-erstone's sister, then you were most likely without perma-nent lodging. It was a small matter to deduce that you were staying at the Langham. You seemed the upper-class type."

"The type? Am I?" she huffed. "And how did you find my room?"

"It was the only room with the window open on a cold night. Fortunately, I'm rather adept at climbing."

"Ah, you're a peeping Tom, then."

"I don't peep! This was strictly business. I knew I was in the right place when I found the handkerchief here on your desk." Modo couldn't resist a grin. Mr. Socrates would have been proud of his line of reasoning. His training had led him to the girl.

"Well, clever deductions on your part, Mr. Wellington. But I'm afraid you aren't entirely correct."

"How so?"

"I had a sniffly nose a few weeks back, so I stole the hand-kerchief from a gentleman whose last name was Longval."

Modo let out a hoarse laugh. "So, perhaps I'm not quite as bright as I believed. Nevertheless, I'm here and, if it's not too much to ask, I'd like to know why I was almost mur-dered. But first, tell me your name."

"You tell me yours," she fired back.

She certainly was brave, Modo conceded. If she believed there was a gun trained on her, she didn't seem in the least concerned.

"It's not Wellington. A little too obvious, isn't it? Or should I be calling you Duke?"

"It's Modo," he said, surprised at how quickly he blurted it out. He chastised himself for being too eager. Why did she make him behave this way?

"Are you *Mr.* Modo? Or are we such intimate friends now that I need only your first name?"

"Modo is my only name," he said.

"Hmm. I see. Well, I'm Octavia Milkweed," she said, "but you can call me Tavia."

"Tavia." He let the name roll around on his tongue. It was from the family name for Caesar Augustus; he had learned that from his studies. It suited her. There was indeed something regal about her.

For a moment she turned her head and her profile in the moonlight made his heart skip.

Concentrate, Modo! He had to get to the root of what had happened to him, but he was growing short of breath and his head throbbed. Under the mask the sweat dripped into his eyes. He leaned back against the wall and rustled the drapes to let some air in. He felt as though his knees would buckle. *I've got to breathe.* He blinked several times and looked through the hole in the curtain. Octavia still sat on the bed.

"Wh-wh-why did you send me to that house?" he asked.

"I can't tell you. It would upset my employer."

"Who is your employer?"

"I can't tell you that either. Besides, if I can't look into your eyes, how can I trust you?"

"How can I trust *you*? That's the question!"

"Perhaps if you look at me, face to face, you will trust me."

Of course, Modo couldn't show Octavia his real face. But perhaps another face, a beautiful one that would please her. He was weak, but if he left his hood on and just changed his face she might—she might trust him. He loosened the mask and began to imagine a knight he'd memorized from an illustration.

"You're awfully quiet, Modo. Are you bored of me already?"

If he spoke now, as his lips changed, he would slur. His chest heaved. Maybe ribs were broken. He realized, too late, that he was making a mistake. The change sapped the last of his strength and made it harder to breathe. He felt himself blacking out.

When he came to he was lying on the floor with a piece of the curtain in his hand. Octavia was standing over him.

"You don't have a pistol," she said matter-of-factly.

"I. Must. Go," he whispered.

"Why are you wearing a hood?" she said. "And a mask?"

"Stay back," he warned. He felt his face to be sure the mask was tight. *"Sray brack,"* he slurred, trying to sit up.

It was too difficult to breathe, to think. He shouldn't have tried to change; it was a stupid decision! The blood was rushing to his head. He fell back again, and for several moments he saw and heard nothing.

"Modo." A whisper. "Modo?"

A touch on his shoulder. *Mrs. Finchley?*

He opened his eyes to find Octavia reaching towards him, towards his mask. She was holding a candle in her other hand. "No," he moaned, grabbing her arm with his gloved hands. "Don't look at my face. Promise me you will never look at my face. I must keep it secret. Promise me, Miss Milkweed. Never. Look. At. My. Face."

But he was weak, and she brushed away his grip and reached out again. "Oh, Modo. It won't hurt either of us. You've seen my face, after all." Her fingers slipped under the black mask and pulled it away.

He tried to protest. "Noooo."

"I don't know what all the fuss was about," she said, holding the mask. "You've got a rather handsome mug."

These were the last words Modo heard before he fell again into unconsciousness.

CHAPTER 15

Tinctures and Whispers

The sack over Oppie's head was tied tightly around his neck and smelled of rotten potatoes. His hands were bound too, and he staggered forward every time his captors gave him a shove.

There were two of them—Dr. Hyde and a man with a hoarse voice. Oppie didn't ask any questions and had long since stopped sobbing. He'd been duped. He knew better than to follow a stranger into a room, but he'd been mesmerized by the clockwork bird. Before he had been able to react, a large man had yanked the sack over Oppie's head and knocked him about until the doctor said, "Don't harm the specimen any further."

Through it all he heard the taunting chirp of the sparrows. He thought of his mother waiting at home for him, wondering where he was, and the sobbing began. Then he was dragged along and tossed up onto a hard surface.

"Take us to Balcombe," the gruff man said, and another man grunted.

Horses snorted and the surface shook, so Oppie decided he was on a wagon.

After what felt to be a long, fearful journey, the wagon stopped and he was pulled to his feet.

"I'm sick o' going down there," a man grumbled. "Not fit habitation for man nor beast."

"It is necessary to have utmost secrecy," the doctor said. "Now, please, do your job."

Oppie was led along for a few yards, then thrown on the ground. The sound of grating metal startled him, but he was even more jolted by the stink that followed. Even the man who was holding him shuddered as he muttered, "Ghastly piece o' work, this."

Oppie felt a heavy rope drop around his shoulders. It was quickly tied, and he was given a shove. As he fell through the air he had just enough time to let out a little scream before he was jerked to a stop by the ropes. The top of his skull struck something so hard that tiny stars glittered inside his head. The smell made him heave. He feared he'd throw up in the sack and drown. He gritted his teeth in an effort to hold himself together.

Hands grabbed him, set him upright in knee-deep water. No, not water, he decided as he took a step. Too thick. Sewage! They half-pushed, half-dragged him through the muck for several minutes. Then he stumbled across solid ground, and a door closed behind them. It smelled only slightly better, wherever they were.

An aristocratic male voice asked, "Why is this boy here?"

"'E's me son," the man beside Oppie said, shoving him forward. "Pay him no never mind."

Another posh voice said, "Why is he wearing a sack?"

Someone cut the cord around his neck and ripped the sack off Oppie's head, taking a clump of hair with it.

"Better, then?" the man asked.

The lamplight blinded Oppie. The doctor looked down at him, his eyes magnified by lenses so he resembled a large insect. Behind him, several men in fancy coats stood at the end of the room. Two were staring at him, but the others gazed off into space. Nearby, leaning over a desk, was a red-haired woman in a black jacket and trousers. A woman in trousers? He'd never seen such a thing in his life.

One of the young men seemed familiar. Oppie couldn't read, but he collected drawings and photographs of the Royals, pasting them to a wall with Queen Victoria at the top. The man looked for all the world like Prince Albert, the Queen's grandson and the second in line to the throne. Why would a prince be in the sewer?

The doctor reached out and patted Oppie's shoulder. "You look frightened."

"I'm not," he spouted, though in truth he was about to wet his britches.

"Good. A brave young man. Now, I have work to do with these gentlemen—please excuse me."

He walked over to a series of beakers being heated by candles. Using tongs, he lifted one, tapped the glass with his finger, then went to the young gentleman standing next to the prince. While the prince's skin was noticeably pale, the gentleman looked tanned and robust.

"It's your turn, Mr. Featherstone."

The young man blinked repeatedly. "I'm not certain I want to drink it now," he replied.

"Come, come, it's a very important experiment. Your companions have agreed to participate and you have already signed the papers. You will go down in history for this."

"Why don't I remember coming to this room? I thought we were going to study the stars."

"The stars?" A derisive huff came from the woman at the table. "Be a man, Mr. Featherstone. Your father would be ashamed of you."

"I'm not afraid," he said, and took the vial, gulping it down. He grimaced and his hand went straight to his head.

A look of absolute horror crossed his face, an expression so hideous that it took Oppie's breath away. Featherstone's legs buckled, but he was caught by one of the doctor's henchmen.

"You'll find your legs again in a moment, Mr. Featherstone," the doctor said, "and your mind will soon be as clear as blank paper."

A few moments later, as predicted, Featherstone did stand on his own. There was something odd about his eyes.

The other gentlemen watched all of this impassively. Prince Albert took his portion next, responding exactly as Featherstone had. Soon all the young gentlemen were seated along one wall, their eyes glazed over. Oppie was surprised at how still they sat. In fact, Prince Albert seemed to have fallen asleep.

The henchman led Featherstone to the woman at the desk. She spoke into the young man's ear, reading something from the papers on her desk. Oppie couldn't hear what she said, but when she was finished Featherstone nodded and stood by the door. He looked, to Oppie, like a dog waiting to be let out.

One by one, the remaining young men were taken over to the woman, who whispered into their ears too. None of them said a word, and by the end, the six stood in line behind Featherstone.

"They are ready to go home, Mr. Fuhr," the woman said to the large man.

He nodded, and the gentlemen followed him through the door and out of the room. Prince Albert, oblivious to all of this, was left sleeping in the corner.

The woman stood and stretched, revealing that she had a metal hand. Oppie couldn't keep his eyes off it.

"Well, Cornelius, seven arrows have been loosed. In this alone you have accomplished more than any chemist in history. I am proud of you."

"It's a small thing, truly," the doctor said. "And we are only half-done."

"Yes. Half-done. You are always dedicated to the task." She shook an admonishing metal finger at him. "You work too hard. But soon we will rest. May I have my sparrow back?"

"Of course." He lifted one of the sparrows from his shoulder and handed it to her. She placed it on her own.

"Ah, this is one of the loveliest gifts you've given me. Do you need help with the boy?"

"Yes, just a moment's help."

The doctor and the woman returned to Oppie's side. The second sparrow still clung to the man's shoulder. Without looking Oppie in the eye, the woman cut the ropes from his shoulders with a knife, then lifted him and dragged him into a second smaller chamber. She placed him against the wall, where she snapped manacles around his wrists and ankles. Oppie thrashed about wildly.

"It's only natural to fear what you don't understand," the doctor said, and his bird chirped in agreement. He touched Oppie's shoulder with a cool hand. "Ah, good, you're already strong and your bones are well-developed. When you tire of fighting me, I will give you some of the . . . uh . . . magic potion that my young friends just received. But it will be a larger dose and it will make you much stronger. I know how young boys wish they were stronger! After all, when England's children rise up to strike against the old black-guards who keep them down, you will need to be strong. So, when you are ready to co-operate, my boy, we can begin."

CHAPTER 16

Secrets and Tales

A cutlass was displayed on the wall alongside a black bear's head, its mouth open in a roar, its marble eyes twinkling in the morning light. Below it was a brass bed, the sheets luxurious and thick. And under them, snoring with a slight wheeze, was Modo.

As he was just coming to, he sensed someone entering the room, and heard the squeak of leather as that person sat in a nearby chair. Seconds passed and then something poked him in the shoulder.

Modo opened one eye, then the other. His eyes focused and widened in surprise. "Mr. Socrates!" he exclaimed. He sat up, ignoring the pain in his chest. "You—how did you get here?" He looked around. "Where am I?"

"You're in Towerhouse. This is one of my London safe houses. I figured it was best to keep you off the streets for the next while. You have stirred up a hornets' nest."

"Hornets' nest?" It took Modo a moment to recall a few details from the previous night. "It was more than a hornets' nest, sir." When he moved his right arm to feel for his mask, he saw that his burn marks and injuries had been covered by a thick, green paste that smelled of mint. "What's on my arm?"

"Tharpa treated your wounds. Some mystical poultice. I'm certain it will heal you—at least it hides your smell."

Good ol' Tharpa, Modo thought. *He's here!* Modo felt his cheek; his face had reverted to its original shape. There were scabs where the woman with the metal hand had scratched him.

"How did I get here?"

"Tharpa carried you. With the help of Octavia."

"You know Octavia?"

"Of course. She works for me." Mr. Socrates tapped the bed with his walking stick. "You should be putting some of this together yourself, Modo. Octavia assumed you were also my agent and that I would want to help you. She brought you here by cab, telling the cabbie that this was the home of a doctor. And you do need help. Judging by your breathing you have broken a rib, but there's no damage to your lungs. You cough up ashes, not blood."

Modo rubbed his forehead and came away with a soot-stained hand. "How long have I been unconscious?"

"You've slept for ten hours. I could wait no longer. I need to know what you've discovered about the Young Londoners Exploratory Society. But first I must compliment you. You have passed the test."

Modo's lips were so dry it hurt to smile, but smile he did.

"I'm pleased by your progress," Mr. Socrates continued. "You've adapted to your surroundings, found lodging, procured a source of income and used all means at your disposal to survive. Perfect. I felt that you were ready for the next step, so I had Octavia assign you a task. You're to be congratulated. The faith that I have placed in you has been rewarded."

"Thank you, sir. It was . . . uh . . . Sometimes I didn't eat so well." He let out a breath, and then, more angrily than he intended, said, "I nearly died, you know."

"Yes," Mr. Socrates replied. "I'm aware of that."

But Modo's anger continued to flare. *You pushed me out of the coach. You abandoned me on the street to fend for myself*, he thought. He sucked in a deep breath.

Mr. Socrates didn't seem to notice his broiling mood. "I cannot resist congratulating myself. Your carefully planned upbringing has paid off. I have taken many notes on my methods and will employ them again in the future."

Employ them again? With whom? Did he have other young agents he was raising? Modo was surprised to feel a stab of jealousy. Did Mr. Socrates like the other agents more? Were they handsome? Beautiful? Modo ground his teeth together. He was being silly. What he wanted most was for his master to pat him on the shoulder. He was reminded of the last person to pat his back.

"Is Mrs. Finchley here?"

Mr. Socrates shook his head. "She has other duties."

Another stab of jealousy! Was she looking after a new agent-in-training? Modo swallowed the lump in his throat.

"Is she keeping well?"

"Do not dwell on her, Modo," Mr. Socrates said. "She has served her purpose in your life. Do not succumb to sentimental attachments."

"And should I forget you too, if need be?" Modo asked.

Mr. Socrates looked momentarily startled. "Well, well, well. You have grown a bit of a spine, Modo. Good. But don't become flippant." He tapped his walking stick once on the floor. "You did fail in one aspect."

"And what was that?"

Mr. Socrates produced a section from the London *Times* and handed it to Modo. On the bottom of the page was a headline: "House Burned Down by Escaped Convict." Modo read the story quickly.

> The house at 22 Balcombe Street has burned to the ground. No one was found inside and the owner, one Mr. Arden Munsen, is away in India, but witnesses saw a deranged convict escaping the blaze. "He was deformed," a bystander reported. "It shall not be hard for the authorities to track him down."

Modo felt sick, remembering how a woman had actually fainted at the sight of him. Then a horrid thought occurred to him: his enemies would read this and know he had escaped. Picturing the red-haired woman set on his destruction made him panic, but he took solace in the knowledge that they would have no way of tracking him and no idea what he really looked like.

Mr. Socrates gathered up the paper. "As a rule, I prefer no descriptions of my agents to appear in print."

"It won't happen again, sir," Modo said. "Next time I'll just let myself burn up in the blaze."

Mr. Socrates actually let out a chuckle. "You are coming into your own, Modo. I am proud of you."

Modo felt pleased.

There was a knock at the door and then Tharpa stuck his head into the room. By way of a greeting he nodded to Modo, then said to Mr. Socrates, "Miss Milkweed has arrived."

"Bring her up."

Tharpa nodded again and left.

Modo was disappointed not to get so much as a "Nice to see you" from Tharpa. Then he realized what Tharpa had said.

"Miss Milkweed?" Modo asked, full of hope.

"Yes. Octavia has arrived. I must say finding her was a fine piece of detective work."

Modo sat up, alarmed. "She's on her way up here?"

"Yes."

"Well, she can't see me like this."

"Like what?"

"I'm not dressed properly." Modo looked around desperately for clothes, wincing as his ribs moved. He threw on a large robe that had been hanging on the bedpost, and his hump disappeared into its great folds.

"Don't be modest, Modo. She's a professional agent. She has seen worse things than a young invalid."

"Where's my mask? I don't want her to see my face." He'd meant it to be a calm statement but heard himself whining.

"Ah, now I understand. You're feeling more than modesty. Well, you should not always rely on your mask. Why don't you just transform your face?"

"There isn't enough time."

"There is if you concentrate."

Which face had he used? Ah, yes, the knight, of course. His bones and muscles knew the face well. He set his jaw, pictured his nose straight and perfect. Just his face, that's all he needed to change. Perspiration beaded on his brow. His heart thudded against his breastbone. He made his nose straighten.

Footsteps echoed in the stairwell outside his door. She was climbing the stairs, talking to Tharpa. He recognized the timbre of her voice but couldn't catch the words.

He lowered his ears and made them shrink, sweat dripping into his eyes.

"You're botching it," Mr. Socrates scolded. "Your eyes are uneven. Concentrate. You've done this a thousand times."

Their footsteps were growing closer. Octavia laughed lightly. Modo hadn't even begun to work on his hair.

"Concentrate!" Mr. Socrates commanded.

The door swung open. Modo slapped a disfigured hand over his face, but Tharpa entered first, then motioned to their guest to stop, closing the door in her face. He marched to the bed, grabbed a nightcap from the desk and pulled it over Modo's head, then handed him a handkerchief. Modo covered his face with it.

"Your eyes," Tharpa said. "Straighten them. Let the rest go. Then all will be well."

Modo caught the sideways grin that Mr. Socrates gave Tharpa.

"You're being overly protective," Mr. Socrates said.

"The secret of his face should *remain* a secret," Tharpa answered flatly, then he returned to the door.

Mr. Socrates shrugged. "Yes. I suppose. The secret is more important than this little test. Bring her in."

Modo finished straightening his eyes and tied the handkerchief across his nose and mouth. How long would his features stay that way?

Octavia glided in wearing a grey dress, her hair concealed under a pink bonnet.

Mr. Socrates took her hand. "How kind of you to join us, Miss Milkweed." He motioned towards Modo. "You've already met our guest."

"Yes." Her piercing eyes examined Modo. "I'm glad to see you again, sir. Why are you covering your face?"

"I—I have a rash."

"Nothing contagious, I hope."

"No, of course not," he replied. Her presence filled the room with light. "I . . . uh . . . I was told you helped bring me here. I thank you for that."

"Oh, you scratch my back, I'll scratch yours."

Modo pictured scratching her back and blushed.

"Please have a seat." Mr. Socrates motioned to a chair near Modo's bed, and she sat down. Tharpa left the room.

Mr. Socrates leaned forward on his walking stick. "I've called this impromptu meeting to ascertain what each of you has discovered. I don't normally introduce my agents to one another, but I have good reason to do so today. I've heard Miss Milkweed's version of events. Now, Modo, please tell us yours."

Modo spoke haltingly, his tongue heavy and his thoughts slow. He felt as if he'd never stop blushing. Octavia observed him like an owl. He began with his arrival at 22 Balcombe Street and described what had happened in as much detail as possible. His nightcap kept slipping, so every minute or so he gave it a good tug. He couldn't prevent the occasional cough, though, and twice had to tighten the handkerchief over his face.

When he had finished, Mr. Socrates asked, "This list of names, do you remember how many were on it?"

Modo closed his eyes and tried to recall the table and the various sheets of paper. "I believe there were eight names, sir."

"*Believe*? We must be certain. Tell us the names."

Modo strained to see the writing in his mind's eye.

"It said, 'Citizens Boon, Saxe-Coburg, Cournet . . . uh . . . Featherstone . . . That's all I can recall, sir."

"Each person on that list may be in danger. Try harder."

"I . . . I can't see them."

Mr. Socrates tapped Modo's leg with the walking stick. "People may die because you have not been thorough enough."

"Chastising him won't bring the names back," Octavia said.

Modo wanted to hug her.

Mr. Socrates gave her a long withering look, but she didn't flinch. Finally, he broke the silence. "Well, Modo, I am disappointed, but now you understand why you must follow my methodologies in detail. Each lesson I gave you had its purpose. Even though you didn't know this was an official assignment, you should have automatically memorized that list."

"I won't make that mistake again."

"We have a partial list. Interesting that it has Saxe-Coburg on it. That would be Prince Albert, I assume, sneaking out of the palace on his own. We'll keep an eye on him. No sense having the Queen in danger, or any of the Royals for that matter. And we'll track down the others you listed."

"Sir, may I ask why you sent me there in the first place?" Modo asked.

"I have many agents who go to anarchist meetings. The Young Londoners Exploratory Society kept being mentioned by the wrong sort, even though it is a registered scientific organization. We were able to ascertain that Oscar Featherstone had recently joined. So we sent you to discover more."

"And I failed," Modo said, putting his head in his hands.

"Don't be melodramatic. There were things you did incorrectly, but you did not fail. Finish your account of the assignment."

Modo relayed the rest of the story, ending with the burning building. He left out the way in which the crowd had reacted to his appearance.

"The man you spoke of, Mr. Fuhr, is known to us," Mr. Socrates said. "I'm impressed that you actually locked horns with him and escaped relatively unscathed."

Unscathed? Modo's aching ribs cast doubt on that conclusion.

"Until about a year ago Mr. Fuhr was a lieutenant in the British Navy. We had just discovered that he was an under-cover agent, most likely for the Germans, and were watching him. In an act of, I suppose, bravery, he kept his battery post during a minor conflict and was struck by an explosive shell that took his arms and legs. He came very close to death. Odd to think that he would have died for Queen and Country, if that were the last we had heard of him. Doctors were able to stop the bleeding and keep him alive. But one night he disappeared from his bed."

Mr. Socrates leaned back in his chair. "It was the strangest thing. How does a man with no arms and no legs escape from a medical tent? He did though, and was outfitted with appendages that I believe may be powered by steam. This technology is well beyond our own. He has surfaced recently in Hong Kong and New York. Only one of our other agents survived an encounter with him—so you've done well, Modo.

"The woman you speak of is another matter altogether: Miss Ingrid Hakkandottir. I have met her on three occasions. She's a Swede, but it's difficult to trace her masters. German? Russian? She may even belong to the Chinese. She seems to move from one organization to another. There's no one more ruthless."

Modo agreed. His eye still hurt.

"Her left hand was made of metal," Octavia said, squeezing her own hands together. "Do you know the story behind that?"

"She lost it in a sword fight on the deck of a pirate ship, of all things. She's an excellent swordsman . . . -woman." Mr. Socrates paused. "Oh, and it was a sword fight with me, by the way. Twenty years ago."

"You cut off her hand?" Modo blurted in disbelief.

His master paused and took a deep breath. Then, without the slightest hint of regret, he said, "Yes. Outside Hong Kong. We had stopped a Chinese junk we believed to be smuggling goods and she was the captain. Even though we had shot her crew dead and she was outnumbered, she wouldn't put down her sabre. She called me some nasty names and demanded I duel with her. I couldn't refuse the challenge. We fought on the deck while my men watched. I was left with a few scars and a punctured lung. She lost her hand."

"A formidable woman," Octavia said.

"She is most certainly driven. I told her to surrender. Instead, she wrapped a belt around her stub, then picked up her sabre with her other hand. She drove me back to the railing, but sensing that she could not win, she dove into the ocean. Naturally, I assumed she would bleed to death or drown."

"Years later I began to hear reports of a woman with red hair and a hook for a hand. Then, more recently, reports mentioned a metal hand. We'd like to capture her and acquire the technology."

Modo remembered the coldness in her eyes. "What is she doing in London?"

"I wish I knew. I will admit I don't understand the purpose of this Young Londoners Exploratory Society. Obviously it's a cover for something else. The very fact that Fuhr and Hakkandottir are working together is worrisome. I'll be commanding the authorities to keep tabs on the young men whose names you've given us. One wonders why they belong to this group. We are in the business of listening to the wind."

"The symbol I saw on the piece of paper, what did it mean?" Modo asked.

"Ah, the paper. That was a good piece of work to hide it in your sleeve."

Modo grinned.

"This symbol, the clock in a triangle, has been showing up around the globe—America, France, Australia. The diagrams on this page are very interesting." He handed it to Modo. "It seems Fuhr didn't expect you to survive your encounter, or he wouldn't have let you see this."

It was a drawing of a series of squares that together created what looked like an odd device. Modo tapped the paper. "The shape is human, if you imagine it with a head."

Octavia was looking over his shoulder, close enough that he could smell her perfume. She poked the paper with a perfect pale finger. "The protrusions at the end of these rectangles, these arms, if you will, look like crab claws. Are they meant to be hands?"

Modo stopped staring at her finger long enough to memorize every detail of the drawing. "And each of those squares has what looks to be a gyroscope. How very unusual."

Mr. Socrates took the paper back. "It's probably some kind of war machine; perhaps a suit of armour that a soldier climbs into—though it would need an engine to power it. Imagine ten soldiers with armour such as this. Or a hundred."

Modo raised his eyebrows in wonder. That would be a spectacle.

"And then there are the children," Octavia said to Modo, who gave her a bewildered look.

"Oh," Mr. Socrates interjected, "Miss Milkweed has pursued a different goal. She has seen one of the feral children, first hand. You remember reading about the beast-like child several months ago? Well, that boy's not the only one. An epidemic, of sorts, has infected street urchins and orphans." He turned to Octavia. "Please tell Modo, and us, a shortened version of what you discovered at Breckham Moral and Industrial School. I may glean more details from a story well told."

"Thankee, guvnuh," she said, her voice a light falsetto. "It's me honour to be jawin' wif you."

"Drop the cockneyisms, Octavia. You left that accent on the street."

"Very well, then." She clapped her hands twice. "Everyone listen to my tale well told!"

As fascinating as her story was, Modo found his attention drifting. He was mesmerized by her face, her quick eyes, her soft lips and the way they moved around her words. Her earlobes peeked out from under her bonnet.

"And then she disappeared," she finished.

Mr. Socrates said, "The subject that Octavia discovered, and lost, I might add—"

"Orders were to observe her only. I attempted to save—to bring her back."

"If you had followed orders, we would know exactly where she was right now, wouldn't we."

Octavia looked away from him in a huff. "Uh, well, yes—now that you put it that way."

"That goes for both of you: obey my orders. You are still far too impetuous."

"Hear that, Modo, we're impetuous twins!" Octavia reached over from where she was sitting and put her hand on his shoulder.

He stiffened. It felt wonderful, but her fingers were almost touching the edge of his hump. Would she notice it? She lifted her hand, but left behind the heat of it to warm him.

"Now, this girl—" Mr. Socrates began.

"Her name was . . . is Ester," Octavia interrupted.

"Yes, Ester. She had metal bolts in her shoulders. So someone was attempting to alter her. From what I understand, this experiment changes the character of these children; they become extraordinarily strong. Ester must have been treated, after which she escaped, made her way back to her home, then the governess tried to fix her without a doctor. But why would Ester want to leave again?"

"I believe they are mesmerized into returning to the place these experiments are conducted," Octavia said.

"Why do you say that?"

"The girl muttered a little rhyme about going back to Orlando. I don't know where or even what that is, but she repeated it twice."

"Maybe Orlando is a person," Modo suggested.

"We'll discover the source," Mr. Socrates said. "Modo, once you've rested for a few days there will be more work for you. We will get to the root of this."

Mr. Socrates stood and tapped his walking stick on the floor. Octavia got up as well and stepped to the bedside.

"It was a pleasure to see you again, Modo. Perhaps next time we'll be working side by side instead of spying on each other."

Modo only nodded, but smiled idiotically under his handkerchief.

CHAPTER 17

An Arrow Strikes Its Target

That same morning Oscar Featherstone awakened earlier than usual. He left his dreams behind, opened his eyes and sat up. He blinked several times, removed his nightcap and got out of bed. His body ached as though he'd been running for hours. As he removed his nightclothes, he noticed that his trousers, which were hanging on a chair, were spattered with sludge. There was a strong smell of sewage in the air. Having been cursed with a weak constitution, he waited for the inevitable bile to surge up his throat.

Nothing happened. Not even a cough.

He chose another pair of trousers, his favourite shirt and one of his many vests. It was odd to be getting dressed, since he would normally lounge throughout the morning in his robe and nightclothes, then dress in the afternoon. Nonetheless, he shrugged on his frock coat and selected a top hat.

As he slipped on his shoes he had an inkling that something was wrong. He thought back to last evening's meeting of the Young Londoners Exploratory Society. The details were fuzzy. *In any case, it's nothing to bother about,* he told himself. It was probably a particularly lively argument over the lifespan of beetles. He and Prince Albert would often have long discussions into the night over such matters.

He ran a gold-filigreed ivory comb through his hair and felt some satisfaction when it straightened with a slight curl above his ear. He wasn't too modest to recognize that he was handsome. He was the son of a Lord after all. At dances he was very popular.

He carried his hat through the doorway to avoid bashing it on the top of the frame. There was an itch on the side of his neck, but he couldn't make himself scratch it. How peculiar.

Oscar walked down the hallway, a continuous row of windows to his left. Outside it was misty, so he couldn't see London. He felt the chill leaking through the windows. Far too cold to go outside. As he had no plans for the day he would have Welles bring the *Times* to the study and would read it while sipping tea. The *Illustrated London News* was also delivered today. He would spend the whole morning reading. First, he would have Cook prepare a boiled egg and toasted bread.

He was surprised when he turned away from the kitchen, walked into his father's study, and went straight to the desk. He hadn't planned on doing that. His fingers found a key hanging under the desktop, his hand unlocked the third drawer down and withdrew his father's pearl-handled vest-pocket pistol, a tiny death-dealer that fired a single .22-calibre bullet. Oscar's mind had become a flurry of thoughts flapping around like a flock of pigeons, but this had no effect on his actions. He pocketed the pistol.

Within moments he was outside the house. He felt the door as he closed it and the impact of his feet on the cobblestone path as he walked towards the stables. He was no longer making choices; it was as though his body were moving on its own. He willed his feet to stop, but his legs rose and fell, regardless. The crisp air bit his skin. He tried to lift his arms, but they remained rigid at his sides.

At the stable a voice called out, resonating in his ears: "Stafford, I must go to the Houses of Parliament." The voice was familiar and so close. Was there someone following him? He couldn't turn his head. "Quickly, if you will." He had felt his mouth move, his lips form each syllable. It was his own voice, but the words were not his.

"Right at it, my Lord," Stafford, the footman, said. And shortly the carriage was ready, the black horses chugging out plumes of frosty breath.

The carriage stopped beside Oscar and he waited as Stafford got down and opened the door. All the while, Oscar had begun screaming inside his head, *Stafford, Stafford, it's me! It's me! Stop what you're doing!* But his lips would not co-operate, and Oscar climbed silently into the carriage.

He rode along, his arms crossed. He heard the voice muttering, "The symbols must fall. The Clockwork Guild sees all."

The carriage rattled on. Oscar was bewildered: he was a rider both in the carriage and in his own body. No matter how many times he commanded his hands to open the door or his mouth to call out, nothing happened. His heartbeat was regular and he wasn't sweating; the panic he felt was all in his head.

He took a sheet of paper from the breast pocket of his coat. It had an odd, yet familiar insignia: a clockwork inside a triangle. He wrote down seven words: *The game begins. The forgotten shall rise.* He had no idea what it meant.

What had happened the night before? It had been a normal meeting, as far as he could remember—but now he did recall being guided down a long corridor sloshing with sewage and, later, being offered a drink. He had refused it. But then he had taken it. Why? The liquid had been familiar; he had tasted it before.

The carriage stopped on the concourse to the Houses of Parliament and Stafford opened the door. Oscar climbed out, looked left and right. There were clerks bustling about on errands, solicitors waiting for clients, even a few common folk. And several Royal Guards. They recognized him. Oscar nodded to one and strode past them all into the building.

His father's secretary, Mr. Ackroyd, was in the office sitting behind a mahogany desk piled with neat stacks of paper.

"Young Mr. Featherstone, to what do we owe this pleasure?" he asked, his pen poised over a document.

"I must see my father," the voice said through Oscar's mouth.

"Well, he's in a meeting. He shall be finished in a few minutes."

"It is a matter of utmost importance."

"And what sort of matter, Your Lordship?"

"A private one."

Mr. Ackroyd nodded. "Then I shall inform him at once and see whether he can break away from his meeting.

Dignitaries from the Fante are visiting. Please wait here."

Oscar waited as Mr. Ackroyd slowly climbed a set of stairs. He wanted to yell out, *I'm an imposter! An imposter!* Instead he twiddled his thumbs. There was an odd noise in his ears.

Humming. He was humming.

He felt pain in his left thumb. Looking down at it he saw that he had carved bloody lines into it with his fingernail. His other hand withdrew his handkerchief and wrapped up the cuts.

As though he were looking back through a thin gauze, the cuts triggered images from the previous night. He had met a woman, a very beautiful woman. And a doctor, whom the woman had proclaimed as one of the most brilliant chemical minds of the century. Oscar had hesitated at this; he hadn't recognized the man's name.

The doctor had offered him the elixir. After he drank it, she spoke to him, but he felt he wasn't the only one hearing the message.

And now he was here. Waiting for his father. Interrupting a meeting that, since Ackroyd had mentioned the Fante, must have to do with South Africa.

"Oscar!" His father was stamping down the set of winding stairs, his eyes blazing. His broad shoulders stretched the fabric of his suit. He used a walking stick, supporting the leg that had been damaged in Crimea. "Why are you here?"

"Father." Oscar was amazed at how hollow his voice sounded. "Father, something very serious has happened."

At this, Lord Featherstone raised an eyebrow. "What is it?"

"We must talk alone." He glanced over at Mr. Ackroyd, who had returned to his desk.

"Fine. Come. Come." His father led him up the stairs which wound past a window and to the next floor. The sun streamed through the stained glass; the shadows cast on his father's face made him look as stern as ever. "This had better be important. I have work to do. You know that."

"Wait, Father."

His father stopped. "You've injured your hand."

"It's a trifle, compared to what awaits our enemies."

"Our enemies? What are you at now, son?"

"We will strike them right through the heart."

"Oscar. What is this prattle? Are you yourself?"

No! Oscar shouted in his head, *I am NOT myself!* But his mouth wouldn't budge. His father was framed by the large window.

"This is for the Clockwork Guild." Oscar pulled the pistol from his pocket and pointed it at his father.

"Oscar. This is a very stupid joke."

"This is for the future."

He pulled the trigger. A click followed. *Click. Click. Click.* Oscar shook the gun, then threw it to the floor.

His father roared, "What madness is this?"

Oscar was much smaller than his father, but he launched himself at him, batted his father's walking stick aside and wrapped him up in his arms. The Lord's bad leg collapsed and he fell backwards into the window.

Oscar could only scream in his head as he clutched his father and they fell three storeys to the ground.

CHAPTER 18

Murder in the Headlines

Modo dressed in the fine-threaded clothes Tharpa had selected for him and spent part of the morning in the turret of the house. There was a circular table in the centre; the curved walls were lined with complicated bookshelves stuffed with hundreds of books. A quiet male servant fetched toast and an egg. Modo pulled a chair up to the table to eat and read. In a short while he heard footsteps on the floor and by the weight guessed the intruder.

"Tharpa," he said, "what have you brought me?"

A paper dropped on the table. "Sahib would like you to read this." As quietly as Tharpa had entered, he was gone.

Modo wiped the ooze from his eyes with a handkerchief, paying special attention to the one that Hakkandottir had poked. His head still ached; his rib too. He looked at the paper. On the front page was an illustration of a broken window on the Houses of Parliament. The headline read: "War Secretary Falls to Death, Son Injured."

Horatio Featherstone, 13th Duke of Somerset and current War Secretary, has been murdered this very morning, allegedly at the hands of his own son. Witnesses spoke of hearing a crash and others saw His Grace fall three storeys from a window to his death. His son, who fell out the window with him, survived. There is talk of a confrontation between the two.

More details will follow in tomorrow's paper.

Modo set the paper down. Duke Featherstone murdered by his own son?

The door opened and Mr. Socrates entered, carrying an alligator-skin satchel. "You have read the article, I assume."

"Yes, Mr. Socrates. It's a shame we didn't know his intentions. I could have stopped him."

"But that is the thing. We didn't gather our information quickly enough. I have failed the war secretary. Featherstone was a good man."

"Why would his son do this?"

Mr. Socrates sat down at the table. "My guess is that Hakkandottir and Fuhr have somehow manipulated the minds of these young men. But this is beyond any mind-control methods I know of. We are searching for others on that list. However, it seems they have vanished. Including Prince Albert."

"Vanished?"

Mr. Socrates shrugged. "We must assume they are as dangerous as young Featherstone. The Prince is the Queen's grandson and, as you can imagine, this has caused some consternation. But I have other men searching for him. At this point we should concern ourselves with the one man we have in custody. By all accounts Oscar Featherstone had no sympathies for our enemies. Our sources are telling us interesting things. The newspaper does not mention, for example, that he was discovered with a gun. Nor that there was a paper with that odd triangle insignia upon his person—with the words 'The game begins. The forgotten shall rise,' written on it in his handwriting."

"What game?" Modo asked.

"It appears to be an announcement. They are taunting us. And judging by their technology and methods, this is a formidable enemy. Young Mr. Featherstone has, willingly or unwillingly, become part of their plans."

"Where is he now?"

"At the Tower of London. Which is why I'm here. Have you remembered any of the other names on that list?"

"No," Modo said. "I—I'm sorry."

"Don't worry. How are you mending?"

"I am just a little under the weather, sir," he lied.

"Well, I'm afraid this is all the rest I can afford to give you just now. I need you to use your metamorphic skills. And we must act quickly."

Mr. Socrates produced a highly detailed portrait from his satchel. It was a Beefeater, posing in his uniform. "You need to take the form of this man. He is Jonathan York, the sergeant-at-arms at the Tower of London. This will allow you to talk directly to Oscar Featherstone."

"But can't you arrange to talk to him yourself?"

Mr. Socrates laughed. "Ah, no. The association I belong to is so secret, few in the government itself even know that we exist. The Queen has a suspicion, Prime Minister Gladstone too, but it's better for them if they don't know too much."

"Does your . . . our association have a name?"

Mr. Socrates let a small grin curve his lips. "Yes."

"I see. It's secret."

"The less you know, the better." He took a step away from the table. "Anyway, tonight the real Mr. York will be sleeping at home, right through his shift. We have arranged for that. You will take his place at the Tower."

After he left, Modo breathed deeply. Every inch of his body ached. Now he must force himself into another shape. The only thing worse than the pain of that effort would be his failure to complete the assignment.

CHAPTER 19

The Tower of London

Modo was crossing London Bridge dressed in a dark blue, red-trimmed sergeant-at-arms Beefeater uniform, the royal insignia emblazoned across his chest. The Beefeater's cloak was thick and the uniform smelled of sweat and mothballs. He dabbed at his forehead with his handkerchief. He had studied the portrait of Jonathan York and been able to recreate his appearance to Mr. Socrates' satisfaction, but because of the burns, bulbous bits of flesh and skin protruded along his forearm. Tharpa had covered it with another poultice and bandages, then Modo had hid it all under the long sleeves of his jacket.

"If anyone asks, tell them you fell at the pub," Mr. Socrates said.

Another difficulty had been the business of growing whiskers. It was the only part of his shape-shifting limited by his age. Until he was older he wouldn't be able to do it, so Tharpa had attached a set of mutton chop whiskers to his jowls. They scratched his face and sweat made them stink

like dead rats. Modo wondered just what kind of hair the
things were made of.

Modo glanced over the railing at the Thames. The lights
of a few boats floated eerily in the water. He'd been on this
bridge before, staring down at the children and women—
mudlarks—who sifted through the mud at low tide for coal,
bits of rope, anything to sell for a penny or two. It was a
hard, terrible way to make a living.

Even though it was nearly half past eight in the evening,
the bridge was crowded with costermongers clutching their
baskets of fruits and vegetables, clerks on their way home,
and couples dressed to the nines. Top hats bobbed in the
crowd. Modo cut through them all. Most stepped aside,
respecting the authority of his uniform.

Once off the bridge, he walked down the street to his
destination. The Tower of London was really a collection of
towers surrounded by a wall so thick and tall even Modo
didn't think he could scale it. The drawbridge to the Tower
of London was down and he entered through the middle
tower. *Back straight!* he told himself. *You're a sergeant-at-
arms. Carry yourself appropriately.*

He marched under the portcullis and into the courtyard
without a challenge from either guard. He nodded to both
of them, but didn't speak as he had no idea what York's
voice was like, nor how York would act.

Modo turned towards the Bell Tower. He'd memorized a
map, but with only a few ornamental lights here and there,
it was hard to tell where one building ended and another
began.

The cobblestones glistened; a soft rain had fallen earlier. From somewhere nearby, ravens cawed. Modo looked up and spotted the white belfry. The only way to enter the Bell Tower was through the building next door—the Lieutenant's Lodgings. It looked a little like a large cabin transported from the mountains. Light shone from one of the second-floor windows, and from most of the windows on the ground floor.

Two Beefeaters stood side by side at the main entrance, leaning on their halberds. They straightened up as he approached, so Modo assumed he must outrank them. He was about to barge right between them, when one said, "Password, sir."

Password? Mr. Socrates had said nothing of passwords. Several possible answers flitted through his mind. *Rex? Portcullis? Long live the Queen?*

"You look a little pale, sir," said the other guard.

Modo made as if to speak, then coughed heavily. In the hoarsest voice possible, which wasn't difficult since his lungs were still raw, he said, "Am under the weather." He spat a gob of mucus at their feet.

"Rotten luck, sir. But you know the lieutenant's orders. No one can pass without first saying the password."

"My mind is addled at the moment."

"I'll give you an easy one. Where was Anne Boleyn beheaded?"

Modo tried to control his breathing. *Slow, steady*, he told himself. She had been King Henry the Eighth's second wife until he'd had her executed. Where did she die? *Think,*

Modo. At Traitor's Gate? No. Beheadings were sometimes held at Tower Hill, outside the Tower of London. But was that where Anne Boleyn had met her end? If only he'd read his history more carefully.

One of the guards was leering suspiciously. He was a hulking brute, head as big as a bucket. His nose had been broken at least once. Moments earlier the fellow's eyes had regarded him respectfully. Was he taking a second look at the mutton chops?

"You'd better give me an answer, sir," the guard said.

Modo hacked again, produced another phlegmy black wad and spat it past the nearest guard's nose, hitting the wall. The guard stepped back. "Where was Anne Boleyn beheaded?" Modo repeated, trying to make it sound like a joke. It was worth a try! "Right below her chin."

"That's right!" The men laughed. "You were playing us, weren't you, sir. A cat and two field mice."

Modo nodded. They stepped apart and he entered, turning back, still smiling. "Just one question. Where is Featherstone imprisoned?" he asked.

"It was you who took him to his cell, sir," said one.

Modo cringed inwardly. "Yes, of course. I wanted to be sure he hasn't been moved."

"He's still in the west cellblock, sir. Only place he could be, really."

"Don't be flippant!" Modo snapped, as harshly as he could.

Their smiles vanished. "Yes, Sergeant. Sorry, Sergeant," said the guard who'd spoken.

He marched into the lodging, turning in what he hoped was the right direction. He was heading west, at least. He slammed through a white door and came upon a hallway. On two occasions he hit dead ends and had to backtrack. He passed a servant, but pretended she didn't exist, assuming York would have done the same.

He found a heavy door and opened it. Judging by the stone walls, he was inside the Bell Tower itself. Maybe Anne Boleyn's ghost still lingered here.

He followed another hallway until he came to a thick iron door. With great effort he pushed it open. Inside, a man sat behind a small oak table. Modo recognized him by his uniform: the chief warder, a dough-fleshed man with a bulbous jaw set in a collar of fat.

"You're tardy, York," the man grumbled.

"I'm sorry, sir."

"I'll be late for my dinner. I don't like cold eel."

"I won't be late again, sir. I promise."

The chief warder stood and handed the keys to Modo. "The prisoners are in your charge. Mayhew will be here at four bells."

After the man left, Modo waited several seconds, then lowered a wooden bar across the door. At the table he flipped through the large record book. It was filled with details about the prisoners' meals and visitors, but nothing that explained where Featherstone was held. The only thing Modo could do was look for him. He picked up the keys and unlocked the door to the cells, discovering a short torchlit tunnel and six jail doors, each with a slot for passing through food.

He listened. At first he heard a mewling sound, some-thing like the barn cat that Mrs. Finchley would allow into the house for him to pet. Modo crept from door to door, listening at each until he heard someone sobbing.

"Oscar Featherstone?" Modo said.

The weeping stopped. Chains rattled. "Y-y-yes."

Modo tried several keys until the lock clicked. He pushed the door open. By the flickering light of the tunnel's torches, he saw a man sitting on a bed of old straw and leaning against the stone wall.

Modo took a few steps into the fetid chamber. The young man's eyes were glinting with tears, and he was shaking. His fancy clothes had been sullied by mud and his head bandaged.

"Mr. Featherstone, I have a message from . . ." Who would send him a message? The Queen? " . . . your mother."

"You've seen Mum?"

"No. I received a missive from her. She's convinced you are innocent."

"But I *did* do it. That's the thing. I killed my own father!"

Modo wondered about the fellow's state of mind. He'd be hanged all the sooner if he kept shouting out his guilt. "But was it your fault? That's another question. Were you coerced? Had you been drinking spirits? Your mother has paid me to get information to give your lawyers."

"I—I was under some kind of influence."

Modo edged a little closer. "What do you mean?"

"I was drugged."

"Was it Fuhr who drugged you?"

"You know Mr. Fuhr?"

"The lawyers mentioned him," Modo lied.

"I—I think you're right. I don't know. I have vague images, memories. I'm a member of the Young Londoners Exploratory Society. I joined because I have a great interest in scientific theories. We had meetings every week. I remember drinking a liquid from a flask; it burned my throat. It was given to me by a doctor."

"A doctor? What was his name?"

"Name? Corn . . . Cornelius. That was it. Cornelius." Oscar laughed.

Modo wondered if he was going mad. "And his last name?"

"Hyde," Oscar said.

"And what was in the flask?"

"A tincture. It wasn't the first time I'd had it, but it was the first time I did something terrible afterwards." He pressed his hands to his temples and the chains rubbed against his face.

"Can you explain what it did to you?"

"I was two people, myself and someone else. And that other person inside me was very angry. I could feel him boiling with it. A woman spoke to me at a meeting, last night, but I didn't say anything back. It doesn't make sense." He struck himself such a blow on the head that Modo shuddered. "No sense. No sense. Nonsense!"

Modo put his hand on Oscar's shoulder and spoke softly. "I know this is a hard time. I feel so sorry for you. But please calm yourself. Much of what you are saying does make sense."

"It does?"

"Yes. It makes perfect sense," Modo offered quickly, though he wasn't certain he was telling the truth. "Please give me any details you can remember. What did this woman say to you?"

"I don't know. Not exactly. She asked me questions, I think. And read something from a sheet of paper."

"What was it about?"

"I cannot remember. Obviously I followed her instructions, though. That's the only explanation I have for my attack on my father."

"What did she look like?"

"She had red hair."

Hakkandottir. She told them what to do and they had to follow her commands. So she was at the bottom of it!

"What happened next?"

"I'm not sure. I went home, went to sleep and when I woke up I no longer controlled my body. I went to Parliament. That other side of me was full of restrained fury. I spoke to my father, but they weren't my words. I—I murdered him."

"You mustn't blame yourself."

"I must! I didn't do the act and yet—I did do it." He shook his chains. "I saw him, broken, under me. I had control of my mind again, my body. The voices of the Clockwork Guild left me, soon after. All I could do was weep."

"You see, it's not your fault. You would never have done this had you been in your right mind."

"Do you think that's true?"

"Yes. Yes, of course. But I need you to answer a question. You mentioned the Clockwork Guild—what is it?"

"I have phrases burned into my mind. *The symbols must fall, the Clockwork Guild sees all.* They constantly repeat in the back of my mind."

"Mr. Featherstone, it's likely there is a scientific reason for your actions. It has to do with how these people have taken over your interior life. We'll do our best to help you prove your innocence."

"Please tell my mother. Tell her it wasn't me. It was that tincture."

Modo pitied him. Here Featherstone had innocently imagined that through the Young Londoners Exploratory Society he'd be studying science and conducting experiments. Instead he himself had become the experiment, a murderous experiment at that.

"You must think carefully. Where did these events occur?"

"We were led to a chamber. At least I think we were."

"All of you?"

"I don't know."

"If we can discover the place where you were experimented on, we can find your father's true murderers."

Featherstone put his hands to his head and closed his eyes. "We went down. It was like descending into Hades."

"Where?"

"It was an abominable place, that's all I remember."

Modo could see he wouldn't get the answer he needed just now. "Then tell me please, who were your companions? You must understand they are in danger too."

Oscar's shaking and shivering worsened. "Mmm . . . there was Roderick Yarrow, Charles Boon, Richard Cournet, Michael Eccarius, and . . . and . . ."

"That's only four. I need to know all eight!"

"Yes, yes, eight of us. That leaves three. Nixon Hales, Henry Glyn and, of course, Albert of Saxe-Coburg. My dear friend."

Modo ran the names through his mind again to be certain he would remember them. "Did this red-haired woman give them orders also?"

"I don't know."

"What about Prince Albert? Do you know where he is?"

"At the palace, of course."

"I'm sorry to tell you he's not."

"Is he lost?"

"No, no," Modo said quickly, seeing that Oscar was about to burst into tears. "He's safe."

Oscar slumped forward, his head between his knees, and sobbed. "I'll be hanged, won't I."

"No! I'll do everything in my power to prove your innocence. I promise. You are not responsible for the murder of your father. Remember that, Mr. Featherstone."

A *thud* against the main door echoed in the cell. "Open up at once!" someone shouted from outside.

"I must go."

Modo closed the cell door and ran to the jailers' room. No windows. No escape.

"Open up!" The gruff shout was followed by another blow to the door.

"I will. I will," Modo yelled. With no place to hide he'd have to talk his way out.

He pushed up the wooden bar and the door swung open, slamming against the wall. A Beefeater entered, aiming a pistol at Modo. He looked familiar. York!

The moment York saw his own face staring back at him, he lowered the gun. "I'll be blowed!"

The two Beefeaters behind him, their halberds at the ready, were equally astounded.

"Who is this imposter?" Modo demanded.

No one moved. York's eyelids drooped. Whatever Mr. Socrates' agents had given him had not yet worn off.

"You! *You* are the imposter." He raised his pistol, but Modo smacked it away.

"See! *He's* the faker!" He pulled on York's mutton chops, yanking him down to the floor. Modo rammed into the Beefeaters, bowling them over, and scrambled down the hall.

He heard a shot as he turned a corner—the bullet bounced off the stone wall behind him with a loud ping. He couldn't remember the way out. He came to stone stairs, and having no other way to go, charged up them, shouts and footsteps close behind him.

He leapt through a window, using his left arm to block his face from the glass as his right grabbed the ledge. He jerked to a stop and for a moment hung over the stone ledge. His arm was weak and his hand was growing slippery with blood, having been cut on the broken window. He swung his legs onto the ledge, straightened and forced himself to clamber several feet up the jutting stones on the wall to the

top of the Bell Tower. He crouched in the shadow of the belfry, to gather his thoughts. The courtyard below was quiet.

Then, right next to him, the bells rang out, the terrific
clang-clang-clang nearly knocking him over the wall. A
clamour rose in the courtyard. He peered down to see men
running this way and that, yelling to one another. Then he
heard the portcullis at the front gate clank shut.

Eventually they would search the rooftops. Better to run
now, especially while he had the advantage of the dark. He
dashed across the tower and jumped down onto the Lieutenant's Lodgings, bounding along the pitched roof. Then
he jumped to Bloody Tower, just catching the very edge of
the top of one wall. By now, all the gates would be closed,
and he tried to dream up a way to scale the walls that surrounded the Tower. Impossible, he realized.

Then he remembered Anne Boleyn and that inspired him
anew. He found a window on the tower and climbed down
to it, forcing it open and slipping into the room, tangling en
route with a tall candelabra. He passed through the door, followed a narrow hallway, then stumbled down a spiral staircase, hiding his bloody hand as he twice passed guards. With
luck and a couple of good guesses, he came across the stone
steps that Anne Boleyn herself would have walked, the steps
to Traitor's Gate, the only water entrance to the Tower.

Two Beefeaters stood next to a boat, guarding an open
gate. Modo ran down the steps, shouting, "He's just inside
the Tower! That way! I'll close the gate."

They ran up the steps past him. When they were out of
sight, he plopped himself into the boat, grabbed an oar and

pushed his way out past the gate, smiling broadly over how easy it had been.

But then he looked down at the water, suddenly afraid. He couldn't swim. He paddled hard to the edge of the moat, jumped from the boat and climbed up the bank to the street.

Minutes later he was charging down St. Katherine's Way and onto Irongate Wharf. He hid behind a large crate and tore off the vest, cloak and uniform. Underneath he wore his thin street clothes, not quite warm enough for the cold night. He shivered uncontrollably and his hand was now covered with blood. At least he wasn't so obviously a Beefeater. He reversed the cloak so that none of the insignia showed and threw it around his shoulders. Finally, he ripped the mutton chops from his face and dropped them, along with the vest and uniform, into the Thames.

Voices cut through the fog and loud footsteps echoed on the wharf, so Modo stayed perfectly still, except for his chattering teeth. He waited for fifteen minutes, and when there was no indication he was in danger of being pursued, he crossed the street, shimmied up a column on one of the warehouses and climbed, hand over hand, up a six-storey brick building, grateful that the cast-iron window frames were so strong.

On the roof he began to run, relieved to be out of sight. He would work his way west and cross the Thames at Blackfriars Bridge. The Tower of London bells rang softly in the distance.

CHAPTER 20

The Association

Modo wheezed his way down the driveway to Mr. Socrates' mansion, past a row of silver-plated lamps embellished with dolphins. Even at night, it was obvious why it was called Towerhouse: the mansion's four-storey turret loomed over the estate.

With each step Modo clutched his chest harder; his broken rib was on fire. He staggered, latched onto one of the lamp posts and rested against it. He wiped his forehead and discovered clumps of hair stuck in his sweat. Bumps were appearing on his face but he had no way to hide them. He hoped he wouldn't frighten Mr. Socrates' servants.

He pulled up his scarf and stumbled to the stone wall surrounding the house. Lights were on, even at this late hour. He pushed the iron gate open.

"Halt!" a voice commanded.

Two large men in greatcoats ran at him out of the darkness, one pointing a pistol. They stopped a good five yards back, unsure of what, or who, they were dealing with.

Modo kept his face turned from the lamplight.

"What's your business?" the one with the pistol asked.

"To see Mr. Socrates. I'm in his employ."

"Oh?" The pistol remained. "And we're supposed to take your word for that?"

"It's the truth." Modo coughed.

"We weren't told to expect guests," the other man said, walking up to him. "Let's get a good look at you." He grabbed Modo's shoulder, yanking him into the light. They were hardened men with scarred faces, but they both recoiled in disgust.

"My God!" gasped the one holding Modo's shoulder. "What hit you?"

"Nothing!" Modo was tempted to break the man's nose. "Nothing."

"Release him!"

Modo recognized the voice, and soon Tharpa was striding down the path.

"Return to your posts," said Tharpa.

"We don't take orders from you, wallah."

Tharpa stepped up and broke the man's grip on Modo with a subtle flick of his wrist. The man groaned and pulled back his arm as though stung. "Next time listen to the wallah," Tharpa said to the men as he guided Modo towards Towerhouse.

"Thank you," Modo whispered.

"They see the colour of my face and they make judgments. We are not so different, you and I."

Modo managed a little grin.

Tharpa patted his shoulder. "You do not look your best, young sahib."

"I'm very tired."

"Well, you have one more task tonight, I'm sorry to say." Tharpa led him into the house and closed the door. He brought a mask out from under a scarf on a nearby shelf. "You will want to wear this."

Modo took the mask and put it on.

With a firm hand on Modo's back, Tharpa brought him into the dining room, whispering, "All the sahibs are here tonight."

Mr. Socrates was leaning over a map on the long teak table. Down either side of it sat five well-turned-out older men, buttons gleaming, cravats perfectly pressed. At the far end was a dark-haired woman in an emerald-green dress. Smoke stung Modo's eyes and he stifled a cough. Three of the men cupped pipes, while the woman's spidery fingers held a long retractable cigarette holder. The table was set with wine goblets, grapes, dinner rolls and sweet biscuits, and littered with papers and maps. The gentlemen's top hats sat along a shelf behind them.

Mr. Socrates looked up, his face drawn with exhaustion. "Ah, my agent has returned. Step up. My associates would like to hear what you've discovered."

They were an intimidating lot, intelligent eyes set into faces that revealed their years and, Modo guessed, worldly experience. Since Mr. Socrates had referred to him only as "his agent," Modo realized his master didn't want them to know too much about him. "I—I went to the Tower." Modo scratched nervously at the side of his neck. "Wh-wh-who are these people, Mr. Socrates?"

"My interests are their interests. You may speak freely."

"Oh. I see." Modo cleared his throat. He felt naked under their penetrating gazes. "I entered the Tower of London as you requested, sir, and interviewed Mr. Oscar Featherstone."

"What details did he provide?"

"He claims he didn't have control of himself when he committed the murder. He'd been given a tincture and it . . . it divided his mind in two. Miss Hakkandottir seems to have planted instructions in that second part of his . . . his self, if that makes any sense, sir."

"Sense?" a gentleman echoed.

He was hunched over, and with his short grey hair and glasses, he reminded Modo of an unblinking owl. He was maybe forty years old, his vest was brown and Modo noticed with a shock that his right hand was withered, only half the size of his left. Modo couldn't help staring at it until a pang of shame hit him. This was, after all, how others always reacted to his own disfigurement and he hated it.

"This suggests personality separation," the man continued. "Did he say who created this tincture?"

Modo glanced at Mr. Socrates, who said, "Please answer Mr. Gibbons's query."

"It was Dr. Cornelius Hyde."

"Hyde—?" Mr. Gibbons repeated.

Modo felt his eyes drawn to the man's withered hand again. He looked away.

"—but he disappeared over ten years ago. He was quite mad."

"I met him once." The woman took a long draw from her cigarette. "Very adept at clockwork and obsessed with hybridity."

She let out a smoke ring that distracted Modo. He'd never seen such a thing.

"Did Mr. Featherstone mention any children?" she asked.

"Uh . . . no."

"Could Hyde really have created a tincture capable of altering the essence of a man's personality?" Mr. Gibbons asked.

Modo presumed this question wasn't for him.

"Perhaps," said a dark-haired gentleman. His well-trimmed, angular beard looked odd upon his wrinkled face.

He was obviously English, but he wore dark blue Oriental clothing that Modo thought might be silk.

"Dire news that he's involved with the likes of Fuhr and Hakkandottir. One wonders whom they serve—how organized they are."

"Well, sir, I can tell you this much," Modo said. "They're called the Clockwork Guild."

Everyone in the room was staring at him now. He felt a little proud to have been able to surprise them with what was clearly important information. He was certain he saw a bit of a smile on Mr. Socrates' face.

"Kindly explain how you came to discover this," Mr. Socrates asked.

"Featherstone said he had a rhyme stuck in his head: 'The symbols must fall, the Clockwork Guild sees all.' And that symbol on the paper has a clock in it."

"Ah, that is indeed good information," Mr. Socrates said.

Modo took a deep breath, flushed with his success.

"So this Clockwork Guild is several moves ahead of us," the woman said. "I want to know how these feral children fit into the puzzle."

"They must be test subjects," Mr. Gibbons said. He scratched at his forehead with his good hand. "The real threat at the moment is this gang of young gentleman killers. And we don't know how many cells of these murderous youth exist. May I remind you that we still have no idea what has happened to young Prince Albert. He could be—"

"Let's conjecture after the interview with my agent is finished," Mr. Socrates interrupted. He turned to Modo. "What else did you learn?"

"I now know the names of all the members of the Young Londoners Exploratory Society." Modo listed them. By the nods exchanged among his interrogators he could tell that many of the names were familiar to them.

Mr. Socrates set down his glass of wine. "Well, better late than never. Any other details you feel should be passed along?"

"Only that Oscar Featherstone is innocent."

"Well, half of him is," the woman said. A few of the men chuckled.

Modo wanted to rush to Featherstone's defence, to press his point about innocence, but thought better of it.

"You're dismissed," Mr. Socrates said to Modo. "Thank you for your services."

Modo nodded and backed to the door, then plodded down the hall to the stairs. A gleeful thought penetrated his exhaustion: *I've now met the elitest of the elite.* They were likely titled, Lords and a Lady, maybe even a Duke or two. And all of them worked secretly to protect Britannia.

"I'll bring you food," Tharpa said from behind him.

"Please, don't trouble yourself."

"I choose to. Your dressings need changing, also." He disappeared into the kitchen.

Modo used the banister to pull himself up the stairs to the third floor. Inside the wash closet he took off his mask. His ugliness never failed to disconcert him, like an unexpected and unwelcome guest. He ran a wet cloth over his pock-marked forehead, enjoying the comfort of the cool water. He cleaned his hands, happy to find that the glass cuts were not too deep. Then he dried his face and hands, and, hearing a noise out in the hall, put his mask back on.

When he opened the door, Mr. Gibbons was standing right outside.

"Ah, I beg your pardon, young sir. The other wash closet was in use."

"You are welcome to this one." Modo tried to step by him, but Mr. Gibbons didn't budge. He rubbed his withered hand. Modo tried not to stare at it again, but his eyes had a will of their own. He allowed himself a brief glance, enough to notice the man's dry, cracked skin.

"What is your name?" the man asked.

"Modo." The moment he said it, Modo cursed himself. He wasn't certain if Mr. Socrates wanted his associates to know his name.

"Ah, I see. Mr. Socrates hasn't mentioned you before. Why do you hide your face?"

"To keep my identity secret."

"Ah, even from Mr. Socrates?"

"No."

"He always has the most interesting agents. To get into the Tower of London is no small feat. Congratulations."

"Thank you." Modo edged away from Gibbons's overly large eyes. They didn't seem to blink.

"Has he told you much about our association?"

"Very little. Nothing really."

"He is such a secret-monger, but it has served him well. I suppose you don't know that two more attacks have been made on senior politicians?"

"There have?"

Mr. Gibbons nodded. "That's why we're meeting. Earlier this evening George Glyn, the parliamentary secretary to the treasurer, was murdered by his son Henry. With a sabre, no less."

It dawned on Modo that if he'd remembered all the names of the members of the Young Londoners Exploratory Society earlier, this man would not have died. The thought sickened him.

"There was also a failed attack on William Yarrow." Mr. Gibbons paused, as though expecting a reaction.

Modo said nothing.

"He is the postmaster general. Very odd target—not usually considered a powerful position. Perhaps they were angry about slow mail delivery." Gibbons chuckled, but even as he did so, he continued to stare as though trying to look through Modo's mask.

"You have a curious name, Modo. Why did your parents choose it?"

"Mr. Socrates named me."

Surprise and delight flashed across Mr. Gibbons's face, and Modo swore silently. He shouldn't be letting information like that slip out.

"He named you? Ah, he has known you a long time then, Modo. In Latin your name means 'formed'—did you know that?"

"Of course." He had studied the meaning of the Latin word, but wondered why Mr. Socrates had chosen it as his name.

"Formed by what? By whom?" Mr. Gibbons asked.

Again Modo chose to say nothing.

"Well, I sense you are anxious to retire, my friend. You've had a long night. It has been a pleasure to meet you." He stepped aside and allowed Modo to pass. "Thank you for sharing your discoveries with us."

In his room, Modo collapsed on the bed. Minutes later he heard footsteps on the stairs and the door squeak open. Tharpa entered with a plate of roast mutton and stewed carrots. Modo greedily took the plate, and while Tharpa gently changed the dressing on his right arm, wolfed the food down one-handed.

When done, Modo lay back on his pillow again and closed his eyes. As Tharpa shut the door behind him he said something that Modo didn't understand. He assumed it was a Hindi word. He hoped that it meant *sleep well*.

CHAPTER 21

A Pair of Wretches

A voice was calling for him, but Oppie couldn't open his eyes. He wanted to sleep for a fortnight. A dull ache was starting to bother him, along with the voice. He tried to move his lips to call for his mum, but they were frozen. Then, he thought he heard his father speaking.

"Boy? Can you hear me?" The voice was louder now. "Please wake up."

Oppie opened his eyelids just a sliver and blinked. He was in a stone cavern, gas lamps blazing full flame all around him. He couldn't move, as he'd been tied down to something.

"Boy! Boy!"

Oppie slowly turned his head. His neck muscles were stiff and sore. Someone was lying near him, but Oppie's gaze was drawn to a glint right next to his eye: a three-inch-long bolt jutted out of his own shoulder! His pulse quickened and he let out a little moan, feeling like he might throw up. Had there been anything in his stomach, he surely would have.

"It's terrible, isn't it."

Oppie looked over at the man who had spoken and recognized him immediately: Prince Albert. He had been strapped to a narrow table only inches away. He too had a bolt embedded in his shoulder.

"We're a fine pair of wretches," the Prince whispered. "They have done something appallingly wrong to us. For the love of God, bolts in both our shoulders."

Shoulders? Oppie thought. With everything he could muster he turned his head to see the horrible truth. There was a bolt in his other shoulder, too. "Who dith dis?" he slurred.

"Dr. Hyde."

"Yerr a printh!" Oppie said. "Printh Albert, my Lord."

"Yes, yes," Prince Albert replied. "I . . . I need your help. They've been giving me a . . . a drink that seems to be affecting my mind. I must escape. Can you move your hand?"

Oppie tried. "A little, my Lord."

"Can you reach these straps?"

Oppie stretched out his hand, but fell short.

"I'm sorry."

"What is your name, boy?"

"Oppie."

"Don't give up, Oppie. I know it's hard."

Oppie wriggled and stretched until he felt a belt.

"Yes, that's it. Pull."

He was able to lift the tongue of the strap enough to loosen it.

"Good work. The Queen will pin a medal on you."

This encouragement gave Oppie his second wind and he loosened another strap. Soon Prince Albert had a hand completely free and was working on the remainder of his straps. Within a minute he was on his feet. He took a hesitant step towards the door.

"Wot about me?" Oppie asked.

Prince Albert looked back. "Yes. Yes." He stumbled over to him. "My loyal subject, I shan't forget you."

Just as he unbuckled one of the straps holding Oppie's arms, the door opened and a man with mutton chops entered, hissing with each step.

"You're awake and undone, Albert. That will not do."

Prince Albert patted Oppie's hand, gave him a conspiratorial wink and turned to face the man. "Where are my companions?"

"They've been released into the wild."

"Well, Mr. Fuhr, I demand, in the name of Queen Victoria, that you release me, and my acquaintance here, at once."

Fuhr's laugh made Oppie's stomach turn. He yanked desperately on the remaining straps that held him down.

"You are not allowed to leave yet," said Fuhr as he stepped nearer.

The Prince swung feebly, and Fuhr caught his hand midswing and squeezed. There was an audible *crack* and the Prince dropped to his knees.

"Release me," he exclaimed in agony. "I'll ask the authorities to be as lenient as possible with you."

Fuhr lifted him up with one hand and set him back on the table. The Prince grimaced, holding his arm.

"Don't you move either, boy," Fuhr said, glaring menacingly over at Oppie. "Or I'll pluck both your arms off."

Oppie stared wide-eyed. The doctor entered, holding calipers and two flasks, while peering through a thick monocle that magnified his eye.

"Oh, wakefulness in both of you. I must adjust the amount of chloroform," he said, shaking his head.

"What have you done to us?" the Prince demanded. "It's abominable."

"Tut, tut, you do not understand. You'll soon be the heart of a giant."

"Are you insane? I won't drink that loathsome liquid again."

"You will," Fuhr said, seizing the flask and squeezing the Prince's wrist until he gasped with pain and drank it, a little of the potion bubbling down his chin. The Prince shook slightly and his eyes glazed over.

The doctor turned to Oppie with a second flask. "Ah, young master, you shall drink your share too. But because you are not yet fully grown, the potion shall change both your body and mind. Tut. Tut. Don't look so afraid. As I recall, you liked my little sparrow. Well, you will become just like that sparrow, except you will be a little god who never tires. And all the little gods and the little Prince will become one god. Do you see? It's so simple."

The words were gibberish to Oppie. Seeing he had no choice, he drank the liquid without a fight. It prickled his throat going down and yet it had a sweet aftertaste. Soon he felt himself floating, as though on a mound of cotton. In a short time he fell asleep.

Sometime later he awoke, throbbing everywhere. Try as he might he could not move as much as a little toe.

"Sit up," a woman said sweetly.

His body responded automatically.

"Look at me," she said, and he turned, first seeing that the Prince was gone, then laying his eyes on the red-haired woman who sat on a stool next to him. She offered a flask.

"Drink this."

He didn't want to reach for it but his hand did anyway, and a moment later the liquid was hot in his throat. He trembled and tears formed. He writhed madly, all the while catching glimpses of his body. His muscles were beginning to bulge, his skin producing mottled, hairy patches. A controlled anger grew in his heart, making him stronger.

When he had stopped convulsing, the woman said, "Finally. You are the last one. We've saved a good compartment for you, near the heart. Follow me."

He climbed down off the table, unable to resist her instructions. As he followed her into a larger room he passed the desk and noticed a clockwork sparrow among the papers. Its eyes seemed to mock him.

CHAPTER 22

Into the Ruins

Modo felt a poke on his shoulder and opened his crusty eyes to find Mr. Socrates standing next to the bed, impatiently tapping his walking stick.

"Time to rise."

"Did you bring me tea, toast and boiled eggs?"

Mr. Socrates laughed. "I see your sense of humour has woken up along with you. You'll be on your own for breakfast."

Modo read the clock on the desk. "It's half past six. I've hardly slept."

"It'll have to do. Two more members of the government have been attacked. One was killed."

"I know. It's awful." He expected Mr. Socrates to blame him because he'd forgotten the names of some of the Young Londoners Exploratory Society. But instead, Mr. Socrates raised an eyebrow.

"You know?"

"Mr. Gibbons told me last night."

"Do *not* talk to members of the association without me.

You are my agent. Do you understand?" Modo nodded, and then, as if to lighten the mood, Mr. Socrates smiled and gave him a friendly tap with his walking stick. "I know I've been pushing you these last few days but we have to move quickly. The Queen is sequestered in Buckingham Palace, under constant guard. She's devastated that her grandchild, Prince Albert, is missing. The parliamentarians are behaving like frightened rabbits. If the Clockwork Guild's goal was to inspire terror, they've succeeded. With the names you've provided, we should be able to prevent any further damage. We hope to discover where Hakkandottir and her accomplices have secluded themselves. Then they'll feel our wrath."

"I understand."

"You and Octavia will explore the ruins of that burned-out house. I've read the chief officer's report; it wasn't near thorough enough. Are you sufficiently rested to transform?"

"Perhaps."

"Do what you can with your appearance and get dressed. Octavia will arrive any minute."

After his master left, Modo got up, his bones creaking. The bandages on his arm were dry, and when he peeked below he was pleased to discover that the scrapes had scabbed over. He willed his body to change, picturing the knight—the face he had put on around Octavia before. It took him a minute to straighten his eyes and lower his ears. Truthfully, he was too tired, but he imagined being able to laugh and talk freely with her. He concentrated until his new face took shape. It was handsome enough, though his eye was still red where Hakkandottir had poked it.

Then he worked on the rest of his body, but the harder he tried to transform, the more his facial features would melt away. He gave up on his body, leaving himself only a little taller and less hunched over, preferring to keep his face perfect. Clothes had been left on a nearby dresser, so he pulled on a grey vest, jacket, trousers and gloves, choosing a camlet cloak to cover it all. Then he went downstairs.

In the kitchen, he found two peeled boiled eggs in the icebox and shoved them in his mouth, washing them down with a cup of cool tea. He made his way to the library and looked up at the curved rows of books. If only there were time to read. He doubted he'd find any *Varney the Vampire* tales or other penny dreadfuls, but it would be fun to peruse Shakespeare again. After some searching, he found a row of Shakespeare's plays and opened a copy of *Hamlet*.

"Oh, you can read, can you?"

Octavia stood in the archway wearing a green striped dress. Modo needed his hearing checked; how had she crept in? The fabric of her long, full skirt shimmered, the light playing over her in such a way that she could have stepped out of a stereoscopic image. He couldn't help but stare.

"Yes," he said finally, "I can read."

"Well, congratulations, Modo." She floated over and grabbed the book from his hands. "Ah, *Hamlet*. He's too much of a gabber, that boy. Wouldn't survive a second in our world."

"It's Shakespeare!" He raised a hand as though on the stage. "'O, that this too too solid flesh would melt / Thaw and resolve itself into a dew!' See! It's marvellous!"

"Marvellously boring. Though there is a good sword fight at the end."

He snatched the book back and returned it to the shelf. "I see there's no point in arguing," he said jokingly. It felt so good to have her eyes on him.

"Did you shrink in the bath? You look shorter."

"Hardly!"

"Well, something's changed about you. But we should go; our chariot awaits." She gave Modo an appraising glance. "I do say, in that getup you look a little like you could be my servant. Will that be the game we play today?"

"Yes, my Lady!" He gazed at her perfect face.

"Good."

She waltzed out of the house, and Modo, scampering after her, grabbed one of Mr. Socrates' walking sticks from the bin beside the door, deciding it would make him look more sophisticated. Octavia climbed gracefully into the cab, despite her dress's large bustle. It took up so much of the bench seat, however, that Modo had to squeeze against his armrest. He revelled in her flowery scent.

"We're waiting," she said.

"For what?"

"For the address of the house."

"Oh, yes," Modo said. "Twenty-two Balcombe Street."

"Don't tell me, tell the cabbie."

"Twenty-two Balcombe Street, please!" he said a little louder.

"Right-o!" The reins snapped and the horses cantered down the wide, curved driveway.

When they reached the street, each stone and rut jarred Modo's rib.

"We're living in some very strange times," Octavia said.

"I'll say. The murders are terrible."

"Oh, that, of course." She waved her hand as though she encountered such intrigue every day. "I was referring to us meeting again. It's a pleasure."

"It is?"

"Yes, well, Mr. Socrates talks about this shadow organization we belong to as if there's a great network of spies like us, but you're the only agent I've ever met more than once. So that's the pleasure."

"The pleasure is all mine."

"Of course it is."

Something about the tilt of her head made him blush. She was looking at his face and seemed to like it.

"I do find it peculiar that Mr. Socrates is sharing so much information with us," she said.

"He has faith in our skills."

She guffawed. "He only has faith in Queen and Country. I believe he's become desperate."

"He doesn't get desperate. He's acting with speed and good judgment."

"Are you his agent or his parrot?"

"I'm not a parrot!" He gave her his best withering look and she responded with a grin.

"Well, any thoughts of your own?"

"Yes, of course. These . . . these young gentlemen have been poisoned with a tincture that makes them automatons.

That's what I understand from speaking to Oscar Featherstone."

"How exactly did you do that?"

"I walked into the Tower of London and interviewed him. In disguise, of course."

She was silent for a moment. "That's impressive."

"You'll find that I have many faces." He couldn't help but chuckle at his own joke.

"So, you're more than just a pretty face." She paused. "I do wonder about these orphans, this business about them being larger, and stronger, and having bolts embedded into their shoulders. It's so ghastly."

"Why did you disobey Mr. Socrates' order and try to take the girl to the hospital?"

"That sounds a little judgmental."

"I'm just curious."

"Truthfully, Modo? Because I was once that girl. She didn't deserve to be part of such a cruel experiment. It's happening because someone thinks she's worthless. Being an orphan should not make you worthless."

You're not worthless, Modo wanted to say. He couldn't imagine her ever being as sad and dreary as some of the poor children he'd seen. And Tharpa had once talked about how his father had been an untouchable. Never seen. Never missed. Is that what those children were?

"I want to bloody the nose of the person behind this," Octavia said. "What's the point of it?"

"Perhaps Mr. Socrates and his associates know. Last night I met several of them."

"You did?" She patted Modo's knee. "Tell me! Tell me!"

"Well, the men are all older than Moses." She laughed and Modo grinned with delight. "There was a woman, too. Not a friendly sort."

"Lady Artemis Burton, I'd wager. I met her once with Mr. Socrates. She's a walking ice sculpture. Did you know they call themselves the Permanent Association?"

"How'd you discover that?"

"Oh, I keep my ears and eyes open. They chose their name because they want to bring order to the world and have Britannia rule it permanently. After all, the British way is the best way."

"You sound doubtful." He stroked the handle of the walking stick.

"Who am I to worry about that? Let the mucky-muck plutocracy stab one another in the backs. It's richly entertaining!"

"What kind of attitude is that?"

"My own. You should try having your own."

"What does that mean?"

"Nothing, guvnuh."

Modo snorted. She was the most exasperating person in the world! "Well, if you disdain them so much, why do you work for them?"

She gave a thin slice of a smile. "Because the job is a brilliant, exhilarating game."

They passed near a park and Modo observed well-dressed boys and girls hitting a ball with a wooden mallet. One girl laughed with another and Modo felt envious. He'd never played games outdoors.

"What are they playing?" he asked.

"Croquet," Octavia said. "Haven't you seen it before?"

"I've read about it."

She went silent, so he turned his head to look at her and discovered that she was unabashedly staring at him. Panic struck his heart: was his face changing? But then she said, "Only read about croquet in books? You're an odd one, Modo."

Before he could respond the cab stopped with a jerk. "Here ye be!" shouted the cabbie.

Modo climbed out, and leapt from the last step to the street, giving himself a sharp twinge in his rib. Nonetheless, he offered a gloved hand to Octavia, who took it and elegantly descended from the cab. He liked how firmly she held his hand, and was sorry when she let it go. He dug in his pockets but he had no money. Octavia smiled and paid the driver.

They walked through the front gate, which had been left ajar. The house was charred and the lingering smell of smoke brought the events of two days earlier flooding back: the mad fear of being trapped in that chair like an animal; the flames leaping around his feet. The stone walls still stood, but the roof was gone. Judging by the scattered spoons, burned boxes and broken chairs in the yard, scavengers had already been through the house.

"You're stooping a bit, Modo. Are you unwell?" Octavia asked.

"It's only an affectation." He had been using the walking stick for support because his body was twisting slowly into its hunched shape. "People underestimate me,

I find, if I behave like I'm crippled." All the same Modo straightened up.

"You're almost as tall as me when you do that."

While they poked through the rubble, Modo kept an eye out for his haversack, even though it likely had disappeared in the flames, along with his spyglass. He missed the spyglass; it had been a handy tool.

He turned over a few bricks with his walking stick, stopping when he found glass on the ground outside a charred window.

"This is where I jumped out."

"You must have been very frightened."

"Frightened?" He waved his hand dismissively. "I just needed a breath of fresh air."

Octavia gave him a playful slap on the shoulder. "You're a right jolly jester—I like that."

They worked their way through the house, avoiding places where the floor had been burned away, revealing the cellar. Modo spotted a half-burned pair of India-rubber boots and the sight prodded a memory. He nudged them with the stick. "Three pairs of boots sat here. And Fuhr had a scent of sewage about him."

"Curious. Most gentlemen don't stroll in the sewer for a bit o' fun."

A curly lock of her hair had fallen loose and bounced gently on her forehead. It mesmerized him.

"Featherstone did talk about descending into Hades," he said.

"Ester may have disappeared down a manhole. It would make sense for us to look underground."

"Will it be safe?" His voice cracked. The idea of climbing into a rat-infested sewer made his skin crawl.

"Safe? Be brave, Modo."

"This isn't about bravery," he lied. "It's about the wisdom of going where we may not be able to breathe." He thought he sounded very rational.

"The rat catchers and sewer workers survive down there. It hasn't rained very much for a few days so the flow should be lower. We don't want to go back to Mr. Socrates with nothing; he becomes such a crab when that happens."

Modo laughed in agreement, feeling a little traitorous for doing so. He gave the boots a final prod, inadvertently twisting the knob on the top of the cane. Something at the end of the cane flashed and sliced the boot in half.

"Zounds!"

Octavia walked over to him. "What is it?"

He lifted the walking stick to find a five-inch blade protruding from its end. "Mr. Socrates' walking stick is also a weapon." He turned the knob back again and the knife slid into the base of the stick.

"That's a nasty instrument. Mr. S really does like his tools."

Modo made the knife eject again and again. "Fascinating," he whispered.

"When you're done playing, we'll continue our work."

"Oh, fine. Where do we go?" he asked.

"I assume there's a sewer entrance in the vicinity."

They walked to the backyard where Octavia explored a well built of stone. Modo looked in the garden shed, then behind a fountain. He crossed the wooden floor of the gazebo and was taken by the sound. He tapped the floor with the walking stick, then again with his right foot, hard. It sounded hollow. Looking closer, he saw the outline of a trap door surrounding him.

As he took another step the slats beneath his feet snapped. He let out a scream, grabbing at the air as he fell. A breathless second later he hit the bottom, jarring his legs.

"Modo!" Octavia was looking down from at least ten feet above him.

He moved his legs, which hurt but weren't broken. He tapped his foot on a circular stone lid, and yelled with all the drama he could muster, "Behold, I present to thee the sewer!"

CHAPTER 23

Underground

Octavia watched from above as Modo effortlessly lifted the stone lid. He was unusually strong under all his oversized clothing, and she was about to tell him so, just to see his reaction, when he staggered back. A moment later a thick wall of stench overcame her, making her eyes weep.

"You may not want to come down here," he announced, covering his mouth and nose with the hood of his cloak.

"Nonsense!" Octavia climbed quickly down the wooden ladder from the trap door, but as she got closer to the sewer hole she slowed. Even breathing through her mouth made her gag. "Oh, nothing like the sweet perfume of sewage to test one's constitution. Do remember, Modo, I grew up in a foundling home. Nothing stunk worse than the governess."

With that she shouldered past Modo and bent over to pick up a rope ladder piled near the hole. "Off we go," she said, dropping the coils into the darkness below. Then she hesitated. The entrance was far too small for her bustle. As it was, it had been marked by soot; she didn't want to add

184

185

sewage to the mix. "Oh, Modo, I can't roam around down there with my favourite dress on." She began unbuttoning her bodice and giggled when Modo looked away. "Don't worry, I have underclothes on."

"I know, I know, but it's improper all the same," he muttered, his face still averted.

"I'm improper at heart. I was educated on the streets of St. Giles, after all." It took Octavia but a minute to slip out of her dress and bonnet, leaving her in a long-sleeved black under-blouse and dark brown pantaloons and stockings. She hung the clothing on the ladder and turned to Modo.

"Oh," he said, relief in his voice, "you're dressed like a boy."

Octavia burst out laughing. When she'd chosen these clothes earlier that day, she couldn't have imagined this scenario. She had simply been preparing herself should she have to run. After the night chasing Ester, she swore that would be the last time she'd give pursuit in layers of ankle-length skirts.

"What's that?" said Modo, pointing at her thigh.

Octavia pulled her stiletto from its small sheath and flashed it at him with a smile. "It's my best friend," she said, and then slid it back into the sheath without looking at it. She had practised this move many times in the last few years.

She eased herself into the narrow hole and climbed down the rope ladder. The hole was lined with bricks that had become slick with fungi. The circle of light from above revealed a half-broken brick ledge beneath her and not much more to stand on. She stepped onto it; the sewage rippled an inch from her toes. *Don't even think about where this all comes from*, she told herself.

She moved over to allow Modo to take his place beside her, but he didn't let go of the rope. He poked at the water with his walking stick. She couldn't see his face clearly, but she was certain his grimace matched her own.

"You're almost invisible," Modo said, "except for your hair and eyes."

"Nice of you to notice them." She imagined he would be blushing. He was such an easy mark. "We need a little light." She reached into one of the pouches in her waistband and removed her pocket lucifer.

"I hope you aren't getting out matches. The gases down here could be explosive."

"This isn't a match, but there'll be a spark. We'll have to risk it. If there is gas, dive into the water; sewer gas rises, remember."

"I knew that."

"Well, here's the test then." She found the switch on the back, flicked it and with a *zap* and a spark, a bright light glowed into life. "Boom!" she said right into his face, giving him a start. Her voice echoed in the tunnel.

"That's not funny, Miss Milkweed," Modo whispered, "and do be quiet. We have no idea how far away our enemies are."

Octavia tried, unsuccessfully, to look apologetic.

"What kind of light is that?" he asked.

"A pocket lucifer—it's one of Mr. Socrates' little gadgets." Octavia held up the tiny lamp, which was hidden inside a pocket watch. She pointed it right at Modo and he quickly covered his eyes. For a moment, one eye had looked larger than the other to her. "It's powered by an electric cell."

"Electric cells can be made that small?"

"Of course. You should ask him for one. He has all sorts of clever inventions. Pneumatic pistols, wireless telegraphs, electric nail clippers." She laughed. "I made up that last one. So what direction do you suggest?"

The light revealed an arched brick tunnel and a long stream of sewage flowing into the dark. Here and there large rats skittered along the edges.

"I don't know that it matters," Modo said.

"Forward, then. Let's call it Octavia's intuition. I guess I'm going to have to sacrifice my shoes. I ain't walking through *that* in bare feet. I'm no mudlark."

She had long ago learned to do these sorts of tasks without dwelling on them. In her line of work hesitation could be death. Of course, she told herself, in this case the smell might be death. She stepped into the cold stream of sewage, teeth clenched as she felt it moving around her calves and knees. It wasn't just human excrement, but anything that could be dumped down the drain. Rags. Twigs and leaves. Fat, blood and skin from slaughterhouses.

In an eddy near the wall, a baby floated, face up, its left arm draped over the brick edging. Octavia's stomach tightened, but a hesitant step closer revealed it was just a cloth doll with a ceramic head.

She held the pocket lucifer high above her head, speaking quietly. "There are miles of tunnels. We could even tramp underground to Buckingham Palace and watch the Royals do their business."

"Don't even jest about that!" Modo exclaimed.

Octavia laughed, saying, "You're from Greenland."

"What do you mean?"

"You're so green you're from Greenland."

"I'm not green."

"Methinks the lady doth protest too much."

"I'm no lady! And don't you dare quote Shakespeare at me. You don't even like him."

Octavia shrugged, tossed her hair back and sloshed on ahead of Modo. From time to time her footing would slip on the bumpy floor of the sewer lane and she'd wobble. Her fear, of course, was of falling over. Lines on the wall showed how high the effluent ran during heavy rains. She pictured a sudden downpour, she and Modo up to their chests in muck or swept away to who knows where in mere moments.

They stopped at a split in the tunnel. Octavia moved her pocket lucifer back and forth. "Hmm. Do we go left or right?"

"Over here," Modo said excitedly. "There are scratches in the shape of a triangle."

Well, this was a piece of good luck. Octavia slapped him on the back.

"Don't do that," Modo scolded her in a harsh whisper. "Please don't touch my back."

She pulled her hand away in confusion, and let him push on ahead of her. She followed for a long time, wondering why he had lashed out at her that way, before she broke the silence.

"So where are you from, Modo? Or may I ask that?"

"You may ask me anything, Miss Milkweed. Whether I answer it or not is another matter."

"It's Tavia," she said. "Please call me Tavia."

"Well, Tavia," he said, and she was pleased that he was sounding friendly again. "I grew up near Lincoln in a house that belonged to Mr. Socrates. He raised me."

Octavia stopped in the middle of the stream. "You were raised by Mr. Socrates?"

"Of course!" He sounded proud. "And Mrs. Finchley was my mother . . . my governess, but unlike yours, she smelled good. Have you met her?"

"No. Is Mr. Socrates your father?"

"No. What a silly question. I—I don't know who my parents were. Mr. Socrates, he . . . found me. Trained me. Raised me."

"So you're an orphan? We have that in common at least. I was left outside a foundling home with just the clothes on my back and a one-word note: *burden*."

Modo stopped and waited for her to catch up. The rats had multiplied, squeaking madly and scattering from the light. "How did you become an agent?" he asked.

"When I was twelve I tried to pick the pocket of an old gentleman. His servant, an Indian, caught me. The gentleman, as you can guess, was Mr. Socrates. He gave me his address to visit if I wanted real work. Since pick-pocketing was a good way to end up swinging at the end of a rope, I decided to take him up on his offer. I still can't believe he paid me to read books, to practise voices—

even to learn to swim, with Tharpa's help. And now here
I am. My boring ol' life."

All the while, Octavia had been flashing her light along
the walls. "Look, Modo, another etching! But there's no
split in the tunnel, so what does it mean?"

Modo sloshed over to the wall and touched the triangle.
"Miss Milkw—I mean, Tavia," he said. "There's something
sticking out here."

"What do you mean?"

"The centre of the triangle is . . ." He pushed on it, and
the section slipped back into the wall. A door-shaped portion shifted out of his way, revealing a hidden tunnel. It had
been set seamlessly into the wall.

"Brilliantly done," Octavia whispered. "Now to see
if anyone's home." She held up the pocket lucifer, lighting the roughly hewn tunnel. It was high enough to walk
through upright. "*Carpe diem!*" she said, drawing her stiletto, and happy finally to be able to step up out of the
sewage.

She motioned Modo to join her against the tunnel wall;
once together they slid along it for ten feet or so until they
came to a large room in complete disarray. Furniture had
been flipped over or broken, flasks had been smashed everywhere, and the smell of smoke mingled with the sewer
stench. A door leading to a smaller room was hanging from
its hinges.

She shone her light to be sure no one was hiding there.
"Lovely place," she said, while stepping carefully into
the room.

Modo poked through smashed beakers and half-burned papers on the floor, using his walking stick. "We're in the right place, anyway," he said, showing her a torn, partly burned paper with the clockwork symbol stamped at the top. She held the light so they could both read it:

to apply the Lycaeunium in two doses a

ount should be equal to 1/32nd of the weight of

ects the conscious personality, which is suspended, and a

alleable but savage personality emerges. Bone density is

harnesses the inner potency! This is the discovery! it

this energy can be directed through a filament to gyro

5% of the subjects die due to organ failure.

"It looks like a portion of Dr. Hyde's notes," Modo said. "Lycaeunium might be the name of the tincture."

"Did you read the last line: 5 percent of the subjects die?"

"It may be worse than that." He held the paper up to his eyes. "There's another number in front of that five, but I can't read it."

"Ah, I don't want to know. Just put it away. The less time we spend here the better."

He stuffed the scrap into the breast pocket of his coat.

They went into the smaller room, finding what appeared to be two operating tables surrounded by trolleys of surgical instruments. Octavia picked up a restraining belt and let it drop.

"Their patients weren't exactly willing. We certainly don't want to be caught by these people."

"Oh, I can guarantee that," Modo replied.

"But why did they destroy everything?"

"Perhaps they know we're on their trail."

She shone the pocket lucifer on a small set of manacles attached by chains to the wall.

"For children," Octavia said, her stomach churning as she thought of Ester.

Modo cried out in alarm as he leaned over and snatched a red cloth from an upturned chair.

"I gave this neckerchief to a boy at the Red Boar!"

"A boy?"

"Oppie. He's such a good child."

"I remember him. He led me to your room. How can you be sure it's his?"

Modo held it up to the light of the pocket lucifer, revealing an embroidered *W* in one corner. "It's for Wellington. I thought it would be a nice touch for my business. Poor, poor Oppie."

Octavia could see he was devastated and her heart ached for him, but before she could tell him how sorry she was, something chirped on the far side of the larger room.

"Did you hear that?" she asked, and they followed the sound until they approached a desk littered with broken flasks. A glint caught her eye and she shone her light on a small metal sparrow, half-covered by a sheet of paper, its head cocked to one side.

"Why, it's a clockwork toy," Modo said, reaching for it. But the bird flitted a few inches away and blinked at them. Modo grabbed at it but it hopped over his hand. "It must be able to sense when I'm too close," he said with wonder in his voice.

"What a clever device," Octavia said, as the bird stared at her light, "but why would they leave it behind?"

"Who knows? Maybe they have hundreds of them." He thrust his hand out one more time, and snatched the sparrow. "There! Got you!" He lifted the bird up and held it out proudly to Octavia, who said, "Modo, a string is dangling from it."

Then something began to glow behind the desk.

"What's that?" exclaimed Octavia.

"Quick! Shine your light over here!" Modo said, dropping the bird.

Now they could see that the string, which trailed down the back of the desk, was burning and was connected to a handful of candles that had been strapped together.

No, thought Octavia, *not candles.*

"Modo," she whispered. "It's dynamite."

Then she felt Modo grab her around the waist and leap towards the tunnel. It was a moment too late.

CHAPTER 24

Missing

Modo felt as though a huge hand had tossed him through the air, whirling and tumbling, as stinging chunks of brick and wood banged against him. The force of the blow sent him right through the open door and back into the sewer, splashing, face down, in the sludge. He let out a bubble, then panicked. Something was on his back. The weight shifted and Modo was able to push himself up to his hands and knees, sucking in a breath, then coughing at the stench and the burning in his lungs.

"Well, that was a piece of luck," Octavia said. She stood close by, well-lit by the flames inside the chamber. She wiped her hands on her pantaloons. "I landed right on you. Very gentlemanly of you to lay yourself down for me. Otherwise I'd be soaked in sewage too."

He stood up and brought his hand to his head. No blood. Flicking aside his sopping hood, he felt water drain down his back.

"Are you hurt?" he asked.

"I seem to be intact, thanks to you." She looked into the chamber. "That was a very clever trap."

Modo patted his body, searching for injuries. His ears were ringing. "Dr. Hyde is the one who uses clockworks. That bird must have been his invention."

Octavia had the pocket lucifer in her hand. The lid was twisted and it wouldn't work. "They broke my light!" she lamented, and tossed it into the stream. "Well, I guess that's all we'll find here." She sloshed back towards where they had entered the sewer tunnel.

Modo paused to look behind them in the burning room and saw, to his surprise, his walking stick, undamaged and floating on the water. He grabbed it and followed Octavia.

The journey back to the gazebo was one Modo would never want to repeat. The pitch black, the squeaking rats and the cold, slimy walls that he had to touch to keep his bearings. He followed Octavia's sloshing and soon they saw a spot of light.

They climbed the rope ladder, then Octavia pulled on her dress and petticoats while Modo looked away. He wiped off his face and hands on a petticoat she sacrificed for the purpose.

"You are a master of propriety," she said, clearly amused.

"It's my nature."

Octavia climbed up the wood ladder first, and Modo entertained the idea that he might be able to catch her should she fall. He knew it was very unlikely that she would slip.

Once outside he took a deep, delicious breath. He'd never tasted such sweetness. He sucked in more fresh air so hard that he started hacking, and had to press his hand against his ribs.

"Are you going to live?" Octavia asked. "You're looking more than a little pale. And what's that rash?"

Modo put a hand to his face, horrified. "Oh. No. Hmm. Apparently bathing in sewage doesn't agree with me."

"Well, it doesn't agree with my shoes either!" she said, pointing down at her ornate shoes, which were now ornately covered with crud. "They're ruined!"

Octavia cursed her sorry shoes, and then they walked to the street. It took wily charm and three extra pence, but she was able to procure a cab, and a short time later the smelly mess of them was dropped off at Towerhouse.

Modo knew immediately that something was wrong. The door was hanging by one hinge and a foyer window had been broken. Where was Mr. Socrates? Modo charged through the door and into the hall.

"Wait, you fool!" Octavia shouted. "You don't know who's in there."

He carried on, picturing Mr. Socrates and Tharpa bleeding, broken, maybe dead. He turned the head of the walking stick so that the knife was out. If someone was lurking in the house, Modo would slice them to pieces.

He burst into the dining room, brandishing the walking stick like a sword. The round table had been pushed over, and the globe broken. Books had been pulled from the shelves. And, blood! Blood on the rug. He ran over to take a better look, but discovered it was just spilled wine.

"You shouldn't simply charge in mad as a Stamford bull."

Octavia stood in the doorway, hands on hips. "Surely you were trained better than this. You could have a bullet in the centre of your forehead."

Modo clenched the walking stick. "If they've hurt Mr. Socrates, they'll suffer."

"Come now, Modo." Octavia grabbed his rigid arm. "Be calm! Chances are Mr. Socrates wasn't even home."

Modo found another red stain on the floor, and this time it *was* blood. He stared down at it as though looking into an abyss.

"Is it Mr. Socrates' blood?" he whispered.

"There's no way to know. But he's survived worse attacks than this. And he would have had Tharpa with him."

Modo couldn't picture anything that could defeat Tharpa, other than a bullet.

"We need to take stock of what happened." She pointed at the blood. "Obviously someone was wounded. If they were dead, I imagine they'd still be lying here, or there'd be a trail of blood out the front door. We can take heart in that, at least."

Modo stared at the blood, then shook his head. He told himself to calm down. She was right. This was not how he had been trained to react in a crisis.

"Yes, Tavia," he said, "but how did they find Tower-house?"

"I don't know. It's surprising they did; Mr. Socrates guards his secrets well. Men like Mr. Socrates have many places to hide. If he and Tharpa escaped, they're safely somewhere else by now."

"How do we find them?"

"There's the rub." She paused. "We can't find them. This is the only house I was allowed to know about, and Mr. Socrates isn't someone you can easily find. He would prefer to find us."

Modo's heart rate had slowed down. *I need rest*, he thought, *rest*. But how could he rest without knowing with certainty the fate of his master?

Octavia sat down on a parlour chair with a heavy sigh. "What shall we do, Modo?"

He turned the knob on the walking stick once more and leaned on the now dull end. He didn't want to sit down with all the filth caked and dried to his clothing. "Well, we don't really have an assignment at the moment. We have no further leads on the young men; one can only hope that Mr. Socrates has located the other people on the list, including the Prince. Perhaps we ought to see if we can locate the missing children?"

"Ah, you're thinking now, Modo," Octavia said.

"What if the people who carried out this attack return?"

"I don't know that I'd want to remain here past night-fall, but I wonder if my room at the Langham is safe."

"We should scout around the rest of the house."

They walked through several rooms, finding no more signs of a struggle. Climbing the spiral stairs to the top of the turret, they discovered an observation room with several slit windows and three telescopes. With all that equipment Mr. Socrates still hadn't seen the danger coming.

They ended their search in the kitchen.

"Where are the servants?" Modo asked.

"They likely fled. In any case, Mr. Socrates kept very few besides Tharpa." Octavia prepared two glasses of water and set them on the servants' table.

"Thank you," Modo said, gulping one down. He touched the teapot that sat on the table. "Tavia, it's still warm. It wasn't that long ago that all this happened. If only we'd returned a little earlier."

He poured himself a cup of the tea, and his stomach growled. In the bread cupboard he found a loaf, crusted with sesame seeds. Mrs. Finchley would have similar loaves ready whenever the master was visiting. He cut four pieces, picked up butter, honey and cheese, and brought it all to the table. He and Octavia ate quickly.

"Your rash is getting worse," she said as they finished.

In all the excitement, Modo had forgotten himself. Now he wanted to rush to a mirror. He felt his face with both hands. Everything seemed fine. It had been only four hours since his last transformation. "I'll look after it, later. Maybe there's an ointment somewhere. What are we going to do now?"

"Well, *I'm* going to take a bath."

"A bath?" Modo couldn't hide his incredulity.

"We need to be clean if we are to take another cab. I suggest, though it may be improper for me to do so, that you too take a bath. You're not smelling particularly pleasant."

Modo made a show of sniffing himself and wrinkled his nose. "A bath it is."

CHAPTER 25

Taff Provides a Favour

The claw-footed bathtub sat in the centre of the room like a luxurious throne, a pedestal gas lamp at its foot. Modo locked the door, then ran the water. He undressed and glared at his crooked body. His arms and chest were dotted with bruises and he had dark marks under his eyes. He badly needed sleep and a proper meal too. Last night he had been in the Tower of London, the night before that in a burning house that had left him wheezing still.

He lowered himself into the hot water. He had never bathed in running water before. At Ravenscroft Mrs. Finchley would bring the kettle from the stove and pour the water into a small aluminum tub. All he had to do now was turn a tap. Mr. Socrates had always had the best of everything, while all his years at Ravenscroft, Modo was left to freeze throughout the winter.

Immediately Modo regretted his anger. For all he knew, Mr. Socrates could be dead, or lying injured in a cold cellar somewhere.

He scrubbed at his skin, wishing he could wash away the hump from his back, the mottled skin from his arms. He floated, feeling as though the hot water were warming his very soul. If only he could sleep here. He glanced at the clock on the mantel, surprised it was only half past one in the afternoon. So much had happened since he first opened his eyes this morning.

After drying off he looked in the mirror on the vanity table. His lip had swollen; his nose was putty. He worked very hard to make his face revert to its knightly form, but the heat had relaxed his tired muscles and he had no energy. *Not now!* he thought. He slammed his fist on the table, rattling a jar of fancy combs.

He threw on Mr. Socrates' oversized robe and wrapped a towel around his face in the manner of an Egyptian mummy, leaving a slit for his eyes. He listened at the door, even though Octavia was taking her bath downstairs in the servants' quarters. Hearing nothing, he opened the door a crack and looked down the empty hall. The moment he stepped out, the floor creaked.

"A bit more haste would be appreciated," Octavia shouted, and Modo nearly jumped out of his skin.

"Yes, yes," he shouted back, and once he'd ascertained that she was actually downstairs, he darted across the hall into the largest room. To his great happiness he discovered it was Mr. Socrates'. He quickly went through the closet and pulled out one of Mr. Socrates' suits. The shirt and jacket were a little too tight and pressed against his hump, and he had to take a pair of scissors to the legs of the trousers to shorten them, but by and large he looked quite smashing.

He hoped his master would forgive the necessary alterations. He went back to the closet and selected a heavy black
cloak with a large hood.

He stopped to stare at his face in the small mirror. It was
growing more disfigured by the minute. And then he saw
something sitting on a bureau just beyond the vanity table
that surprised and delighted him. On a wooden stand was
a flesh-coloured mask he had worn a few years earlier. He
touched it lightly.

What did it mean? Was Mr. Socrates so proud of him
that he kept this memento with all his most personal belong-
ings? Or was he perhaps just proud of his ability to mould
young people to his will? Next to the mask was a portrait
of a woman wearing a red dress. Was Mr. Socrates married?
He found it impossible to imagine. Yet, here was a woman,
and beside her picture, a dried rose. And a bracelet small
enough for a baby. For a moment Modo allowed himself to
imagine it had been his own bracelet.

Modo plucked up the mask and was amazed that it still
fit, though perhaps a little too snugly. He opened a drawer
and found a pair of thin kid gloves and a belt with pouches,
each one holding a different item: a small knife, a pocket
lucifer, a wire with a small hook and a fountain pen. He was
about to push the unusual button on the pen, but decided
against it in case it sprayed ink. He buckled the belt under
the suit jacket. After checking his mask in the mirror, Modo
tightened the cloak's hood and pulled on the gloves.

He was exhausted, but made his way back to the bath-
room and found the torn piece of paper that Dr. Hyde had

written on, and tucked it in a pocket. He went to the front door where Octavia was waiting. Her hair was still damp and she was tying it back.

"You're wearing a disguise again, I see. A bout of shyness?"

"No, the rash is worse, that's all."

"You're a very odd man, Modo. And you seem shorter." Modo stood up as tall as he could. "Well, that's better," she said, and stopped fussing with her hair. "While you've been playing dress-up, I've come up with a plan. But first we must hurry down to Berkeley for a cab. No time to talk now."

They arrived on Berkeley Street breathless, and Octavia hailed a cab. She gave the driver an address near Seven Dials.

"Why there?" Modo asked.

"At other times, when needed, I have relied on contacts from my old life."

"Your old life?"

"My time as a pickpocket and grifter."

"And you still have dealings with these thieves?" Modo blurted.

"Why are you so judgmental?"

"I'm not judgmental!"

This prompted a snort from Octavia. "Who did you play with to make you behave this way?" she asked.

"I didn't play. I never left the house."

"You never left the house? Ever?"

"Not until six months ago."

She actually looked concerned—maybe even sad. "That's terribly cruel."

"No. No. Mr. Socrates was training me to be an agent."

"How many years were you there?"

"Thirteen."

"Thirteen years!" Her eyes flashed.

"He saved me," Modo said weakly. But he knew she was, at least in part, right. It was where his own anger was rooted. There was so much more he would have learned had he been allowed to live a real life.

Octavia went on: "Saved you from what, Modo?"

Of course, he couldn't tell her that. Mr. Socrates had told him that he was such a deformed child the orphanage sold him to gypsies and they made a profit from displaying his ugliness in a travelling grotesqueries show. "He just did. You must believe me."

"He's not much better than this Dr. Hyde, then."

"Mr. Socrates is kind to you and to me!"

"For his own purposes, yes."

"No, he . . . he . . ." And Modo nearly said the words *loves me*. But he had no way of knowing that.

"This is confounding you, Modo. I'm sorry but I do like to speak my mind. It would be best if you got used to it."

He glared at her, but he didn't imagine she could measure his anger through the mask. The way she sat with her back so straight, her face so haughty, infuriated him. How dare she speak of Mr. Socrates that way, after all the master had done for her. For him. For Britain.

"Are you done sulking?" she asked, as the Hansom cab pulled to a stop. "If not, you can stay here." She climbed out and paid the driver.

Modo leapt down from his side. Octavia had already gone on ahead and crowds of muffin men and vagabonds were closing in around her. It was mid-afternoon, and they hoped to sell their wares to sailors and other workers going to or coming from the docks. Modo snapped his head to the left and right, searching for Octavia, his heart beating wildly. He glanced at the nearest rooftop, every nerve shouting for him to flee the hordes. He'd been in this section of St. Giles before, but always on a rooftop. People jostled him; someone's elbow nearly knocked his mask off.

Then, through a break in the crowd, he spotted Octavia striding away from him. Modo ran for a breathless minute and caught up with her.

"Don't dawdle," she said.

"Don't walk so fast!"

She stopped in front of a child, his unkempt hair the colour of coal, his shirt more holes than thread. The boy's eyes flitted back and forth between Modo and Octavia.

"Take me to Taff," she said.

"Taff ent just seein' nobody," he replied. "You wait 'ere, I'll ask 'im 'bout an audience." He darted off, slipping into the crowd like a weasel into a hole, and came back a few minutes later with an older boy, who said, "Mr. Taff will see you now." The older child led the three of them down a narrow alley. They passed doors crowded with half-crazed-looking men, thin and pale.

"Opium dens," Octavia said matter-of-factly.

Modo had heard about these places. Men smoked the

substance and it turned them into monsters; that was how Mrs. Finchley had explained it.

The boys led them into an ancient lodging house. The timbers had shifted so that the frame was at a precarious angle and the rotted door swung on one hinge. Inside were several tables; an old man sat at one of them. At the sight of Octavia he stood and walked towards her, every second step thumping loudly on the slatted floor. When the man got around the table, Modo could see that he had a wooden leg. He held a mug that sloshed with beer.

"Old Taff thought it were a lady come to visit." The man had a grey-black beard and fiery eyes. "But it's just my dear ol' Octavia. And look at you, all fancied up and haristocratic, I see. And who's his Lordship beside 'er?"

"My companion's name is Modo."

"Oh, and listen to you! Speaking all refined and like that. Who you calling friend these days, I wonder?"

Octavia rolled her eyes.

"Oh, I know, I know," Taff continued, "the words is you keep interesting company these days, including this man. Pray tell, why the mask?"

Octavia replied before Modo had a chance. "He's a frowner. It makes his face look rather nasty."

Modo stiffened.

Taff nodded, gave Modo a wink. "I should wear a mask too. Me figurehead ain't so pleasant. Neither's the rest of me." He tapped his wooden leg and chortled. "Suppose you're wondering where my good leg went? Well, lad, it's shark food. Lost it to a cannonball in service of 'er Majesty.

A cryin' shame. Me boys are me legs now." He took a chug from his beer. "Well, Octavia, as always Ol' Taff is 'appy to see you. None of these scabs could match your skill. You be lookin' for employment, then?"

She laughed lightly. "It's wisest to leave that business once one reaches hanging age. Garret taught me that."

Taff nodded. "'Is death still makes me 'art 'eavy. I miss that lad."

"Yes, and well you should," she said, rather coldly. "I've come for a favour."

"A favour?" Taff rubbed his hands together. "Yes, I so enjoy providin' favours."

"I need you to tell me what you know about all the missing children."

"The inspectors don't want to talk about it, but me business is hurting. I've lost several of me mob already."

"Did you ever find any of them again?"

"One boy, Willie, and 'e told tales of labourin' under the ground in tunnels. Then 'e went yellow and died. I think 'is insides stopped workin'."

Modo imagined Oppie dying the same hideous way. "Who's behind the kidnappings?" he asked.

"Oh, so 'e speaks, does 'e?" Taff said with a sneer.

"Yes, and he asked an important question," Octavia said.

"I can only tell you that the papers are wrong. The number of urchins who've disappeared is much higher. None of my riff-raff will go to work at night any more. I cain't say I blames 'em. I'd go meself, but for this gammy leg. Lost it to a cannonball, you know."

"You mentioned that," Modo said.

"Did I? Hmm. Must be goin' balmy, eh?"

"Where did you find that boy? Willie?" Octavia asked.

"The other boys found 'im near a boarded-up train tunnel entrance on Fleet Lane. Closed to the public, if you gets me meaning."

"I do," Octavia said.

"And that will be one favour owed." There was a gruffness in his voice and a sly glint in his eye. "I shall remember that, Octavia."

CHAPTER 26

The Heart Cog

Oppie did not rest or even stop to eat. His body followed the commands of the men in greatcoats, shovelling coal from the rail cart into a huge burning furnace. Other men melted metal and hammered it into shapes on several anvils. When the cart was empty, Oppie would walk down the track and, along with several other children, drag the next cart into place and begin to shovel again.

Once he slipped on loose coal and fell onto his back without a sound, despite the excruciating pain. He'd been instructed not to make any noise, and so he didn't.

It was while lying on his back that he first saw the roof of the large cavern, lines of gas lights hanging from wires stretched wall to wall, scaffolding reaching to the top. For a brief time, he was able to control his hand. He stared at his palm. It was blistered and black with coal dust. He turned it over to see hairs growing across the back. Then he found he could turn his other hand over and, realizing that he had control of part of his body again, he thought about running.

Yes, if only he could make his legs move, he could roll over and run. He touched the bolts in his shoulders and began to moan. Then one of the guards shouted and the doctor brought more of the burning drink. His body went back to its task.

Sometime later the doctor stood beside him, saying, "You're my creation now. Come with me."

He led Oppie along a metal framework, past the machine the children had helped construct. Oppie didn't understand what it was. It had arms at least fifteen feet long—but what would it lift?

"You will have a very special place," the doctor told Oppie.

They climbed a ramp and walked across the machine. Spread out flat below their feet were many metallic rectangular boxes, like small coffins, with manacles chained inside each one. Dr. Hyde told Oppie to lie down in one of the rectangles with his back on a leather hammock. A large man leaned over, grunting as he attached Oppie's shoulder bolts to the rectangle and tightened them in place with a wrench. He then snapped Oppie's feet into manacles.

"This will keep you steady," the doctor said, "for you'll be shouldering a heavy load." He showed Oppie two wires. They were attached to a hand-sized gyroscope above his head. "The filaments will send you messages only your muscles will understand and will draw from your inner energy."

He clamped a wire to each of Oppie's bolts and the filaments immediately began to glow. Sparks flew and Oppie felt his muscles tighten. The gyroscope above his head began to spin.

"It is set properly. Good."

The doctor patted his arm. "I know, it's hard to understand, but I'm proud of you and all your brothers and sisters. The mind . . . the mind is turning out to be more powerful than even I had understood it to be, and, in the end, it is the mind that will bring this whole machine to life."

The doctor left, and Oppie could only stare upwards. He wanted to shout, *Let me go*, but it was impossible.

Two men stepped over him, grunting, carrying a body. The body's head flopped forward and Oppie found himself looking right into the glazed eyes of Prince Albert. The Prince showed no hint of recognizing him or even being aware of his surroundings. They lowered him out of Oppie's sight, but by the tightening of screws, he guessed they were bolting him to the machine.

"What? What is this?" Prince Albert slurred.

"Ah, enough, tut, tut." It was Dr. Hyde's voice. "More of the potion. It will make you feel better." This was followed by a gurgling sound and a cough. "You will be the heart cog, Your Highness," the doctor explained. "I'm so proud of you. I'm so very proud of all of you."

CHAPTER 27

Into Orlando

It wasn't until Modo and Octavia had walked several streets past the rookeries and rotting inns of St. Giles that they found a cabbie who was been brave enough to drive through the most dangerous parts of London. Once in the cab they bumped and jostled along, eventually passing better streets and then Newgate Prison. The sight of the massive stone building turned Modo's imagination to the many criminals trapped within it, pacing their cells, dreaming of the murders they'd commit once released. He scolded himself. Some might be as innocent as Oscar Featherstone. The poor young man was likely pacing the floor himself at the edge of madness by now. Newgate Prison was where Featherstone would be taken to be hanged. Which reminded Modo of something else.

"May I ask you a question?" he said.

Octavia grinned. "May I tell you a lie?"

He faked a chuckle, found his throat was dry. "Who was Garret? You and Taff referred to him."

Her smile faded and her eyes hardened. "A mate. He looked out for me."

"Why was he hanged?"

"He was caught stealing a pocket watch. A pocket watch is worth a life, that's what the haristocrats think. Didn't take long for them to decide he was guilty either. Next thing we knew, ol' Garret was dancing upon nothing." Her eyes teared up and she dabbed at them with her fingertips. "I watched him hang. All of us mates went to wish him well. It was one of the last public hangings. I was eleven. I learned something that day."

"What?"

"You don't want to know."

Modo did want to know, but the look in her eyes made him hesitate to pursue it any further.

The cab let them off at Fleet Lane. The sidewalk was crammed with people who were certainly better dressed than the denizens of St. Giles, but they didn't seem to care who they bumped into. A few stared at Modo, and he wondered if it was because they were amazed that he was with such a beautiful young woman. Or was it just the mask? *I could take it off*, he thought. *That would give them something to look at.*

At the far end of Fleet Lane they came to a round two-storey building built of bricks. At one time it had been the entrance to an underground railway. The afternoon sun lit the top of it, making the bricks glow. The door was nailed shut with several boards.

"This is the entrance Taff spoke of," Octavia said, "but we won't be going in that way." They walked around back.

"See the window?" Octavia pointed at it. "Show me how you can jump, Modo."

"I don't do tricks," he replied, "at least not without double pay."

He looked up and down the street for witnesses, then used a few overhanging bricks to climb to the window. As he squeezed himself into the tiny frame he wished he had a child's body. He worried he would be stuck here with his buttocks hanging in the air. The ridiculous image gave him the strength he needed to yank himself through to the inside.

He stepped down onto a support timber and lowered himself to the floor. Then he followed a set of stairs to the front door and shouldered it open wide enough for Octavia to enter.

"You're a thumping big man," she said, squeezing his arm.

Modo shrugged.

A gold-lettered sign said: ENTRANCE TO ORLANDO RAILROAD, 1870. Whoever had built this, Modo realized, had expected thousands of customers a day. Now, only two short years later, they were rewarded with spiderwebs.

Octavia stood under the sign, staring up at it. "Well, I'll be."

"You'll be what?"

"The girl I found—Ester—kept saying, 'Must go back to Orlando.' It was like a poem. And this is Orlando Railroad. I think we're on the right track, mate."

Modo nearly fell over. She'd called him *mate*. It felt good. No, it felt wonderful.

Modo dug the pocket lucifer out of his belt pouch and held it high enough to see down an impressive spiral stairwell.

"Glad you found us another lucifer," Octavia said.

"Me too. It means I get to lead."

The air grew colder and soon all he heard was his own wheezy breathing and Octavia's footsteps behind him. "Someone spent a lot of money to have these steps carved," he said. "They're marble, for heaven's sake."

At the bottom, they pushed through creaking turnstiles, passed a ticket booth and stepped onto a platform for an underground train. The black-and-white marble tiled floors were layered with dust. A few rats skittered away, and Modo let his light follow them, until a pair of human boots were caught in the beam. He stepped back against the wall and pulled Octavia along with him.

"We have a visitor," Modo hissed.

"Where?"

"There!" Modo moved the light up from the intruder's feet.

"He's not moving," she whispered.

"No. But he must surely see my light. Should I put it out?"

"Too late." She slapped Modo's back. "I know him!" She dashed up to the figure. "You should too."

"Wait!" Modo said, running after her.

"The Duke of Wellington, I presume," she said, hanging from the figure's arm.

It was a statue of Arthur Wellesley, the Duke of Wellington, standing as though waiting for the next train. Modo's laughter echoed down the tunnel. He slapped his hand to his mouth.

Octavia pushed herself off the statue. "I feel no pity for
the rich fool who'd spend a fortune on statues to impress
travellers, before even building the tracks."

From the edge of the platform, Modo looked down the
tunnel and pictured travelling through it by train. If there
were a fire, passengers would be trapped under tons of earth
and rock.

They found steps leading down to the tracks and walked
silently for a few minutes on the rails. The smooth rock floor
became jagged. A sudden ear-splitting scraping noise made
them both shudder.

"Put out the light," Octavia whispered between scrapes.

Modo clicked off the pocket lucifer and was able to see
a dull light in the distance. They quietly walked towards
it, scrambling over old railway ties that had never been
laid. The light grew brighter and it became clear that they
were approaching an adjoining tunnel that crossed the
one they were in, forming a *T*. Meanwhile the tunnel in
which they were walking had become so narrow that they
had to follow one behind the other, with Modo in the
lead. Now they could hear the hammering and squealing
of machinery.

They stopped, staying in the shadows, and observed the
set of tracks in the crossing tunnel. Three children slouched
past them; they were small, but well muscled and hunched
over. Ropes had been tied to the bolts in their shoulders and
they were pulling a small trolley filled with metal bars along
the rails. Two men in greatcoats guarded them.

"They're using them as mules," Octavia whispered.

"They seem to be building something," Modo said as another cart passed. "The carts are full of metal bars and gears. And there's coal too."

In all, nine children passed them.

Modo tapped Octavia's shoulder and pointed at two large dogs walking alongside the third cart. The nearest hound turned his massive head ever so slowly towards them, and stopped. Modo held his breath. Then, the hound turned and walked farther into the tunnel. The other followed. In a minute the tunnel was quiet again.

Octavia patted his shoulder and motioned for them to move forward. Modo crept a few feet along and checked both ways at the opening. Gas lights dangled from lines on the ceiling. The crossing tunnel seemed new. It stretched to his right for a hundred yards. In the opposite direction the tunnel ended at a set of large loading doors. On the other side of the doors a foghorn echoed.

"It must open onto the Thames," he said. "Come on."

They stepped out into the tunnel, keeping to the shadows, moving towards the loading doors. There was a small door off to one side, so Modo bent close to it and listened. Seagulls. He opened the door an inch.

Fuhr stood only a few feet away, exhaling cigar smoke. Modo glimpsed the wrought-iron arches of Blackfriars Bridge. They had travelled farther underground than he'd imagined. He backed away, pulled the door closed and put a gloved finger to his lips.

Once they had snuck back past where they had come in, Modo whispered, "Fuhr was there."

"Ah, wonderful," she said sarcastically. "What are they up to?"

The possibilities were endless. At the very least they must be creating something destructive. What would they make under the city, hidden from the eyes of the police and Parliament?

"A giant gun?" Modo finally said.

"But surely a gun could be manufactured somewhere else."

Modo glanced back to be sure the door hadn't opened. At least he'd hear Fuhr coming, hissing and spraying like a teakettle. A clanging of hammers was building at the far end of the tunnel.

"At least we know what they're doing with the children," he said. "Slave labour. Now what is it they're being made to build?"

"And how will we stop it?" Octavia added, searching the eyeholes of his mask.

Modo allowed himself the luxury of studying her eyes. Even in the dull light they sparkled. He gave his head a shake and said, "I guess that means we'll have to see where this track takes us."

CHAPTER 28

The Chamber

In the end, it was Modo who came up with the most useful idea. They couldn't just saunter down the tunnel; it was lit too well. So, hanging upside down, clinging with his hands and knees to the beams, Modo crawled along the ceiling, high enough that the gas lights couldn't illuminate him. It took all his skill and remaining strength to inch along. The mask had slipped so that one eye was pinched closed. There was no place to rest, and he couldn't look back to where Octavia waited for his hand signal to follow him.

Where the tunnel curved he lowered his hand near a gas light, and waved, hoping she would see that it was safe to come this far, at least. He rounded the corner and the light was brighter. Looking at everything upside down made his eyes sore.

The tunnel opened into a huge cavern carved out of the earth and rock under London. Here and there forges burned as blacksmiths hammered on metal, steam rising from their cooling troughs. Near one fire a long line of children stood next to rows of metal boxes. Along the far side, at the end of the track, was a passenger car.

Modo motioned again to Octavia. A minute later she was at the edge of the cavern, crouched behind an empty trolley.

"Are you up there, Modo? I can't see you," she whispered.

"I'm here."

"Can you see what's going on?"

"They're making the children lie down in metal beds." It didn't make any sense to Modo. "A hundred or more children. And they seem to be clamping them in somehow. And running wires here and there."

A flash of red hair. Even at this distance he felt a chill. "That woman, with the red hair, that's Hakkandottir."

"She's very pretty," Octavia murmured.

"Her heart isn't." Modo was shaking, having held himself aloft for so long. He heard a hiss, but he couldn't see or tell which direction it came from.

A second figure was clear in the distance. A man with white hair, wearing a white apron. It must be Dr. Hyde. He was making the children drink from a flask, one by one.

Modo could see only part of the structure that they were being attached to.

There was another loud hiss and Octavia let out a surprised cry. Modo twisted around to see Fuhr holding her by her hair. Two more men, nearly as large as Fuhr, joined him. A hound snapped at her until Fuhr bellowed, "Stop!" The dog immediately obeyed.

Why didn't it bark? Modo wondered. Then the answer came to him. The doctor must have removed its vocal cords.

They weren't guard dogs, they were killers.

Octavia kicked Fuhr's leg. It clanged, she grunted.

"A sneaky little rat," he chided. "What are you doing here, missy?"

"Looking for roasted nuts," she said.

Modo inched across the beam, hoping to drop down and save her. He would at least have the element of surprise on his side.

"All by yourself, are you?" Fuhr growled suspiciously.

"Yes. Just lost."

"People don't come this far down these tunnels without a purpose."

Modo would have to shimmy closer and time his drop perfectly. But before he could move, Octavia shot him a look that he assumed meant: stay where you are.

"What you looking at?" Fuhr grumbled.

Modo hugged the beam and held his breath as Fuhr's eyes passed by him. He watched as Fuhr yanked Octavia into the cavern, following the tracks towards the passenger car.

Modo cursed. If only he'd acted, he could have beaten them! But he had to admit: Fuhr was more than he could handle. Add a dog and two henchmen and it would have been impossible.

Octavia was gone. How on earth to rescue her? He stayed still for a time, trying to figure out his course of action. If he retreated, there was no guarantee that he could find Mr. Socrates. Even if he could find him, would Mr. Socrates deem a rescue necessary? Of course he would. It was Octavia.

Modo decided to continue crawling upside down along the crossbeam to the edge of the tunnel.

A dog was guarding the entrance. Its ears flicked. Modo stayed perfectly still as, hackles raised, it sniffed in a circle right below him. It settled a few feet away, and eventually Modo felt safe enough to move. When he couldn't go any farther without dropping down, he stopped.

Scaffolding was rigged along the high walls. Hammers banged on metal, their echoes filling the cavern. He spied a spot where he could leap across and land on a darkened platform. He'd be hidden by the height of the platform and shadows, and glean a better view.

But the distance meant he had to leap. If anyone happened to be looking that way, or the dog heard him, he was doomed.

Arms, he thought, *be strong!* He lowered his legs and swung himself back and forth a couple of times, letting go at the end of his arc. He hit a rock wall, but kept his balance when he landed on the platform. He thanked Tharpa, silently, for all the training.

He got his first right-side-up look at the chamber. Gas lights were strung both across the ceiling and closer to the ground, illuminating the metalwork. How many children were lying down in perfectly fitted frames, one next to the other? Several tall men were with the doctor, moving from child to child. They leaned over and attached each child to a compartment with large iron wrenches. The bolts in the children's shoulders held them in position. The structure had a few higher extensions and large rectangular protrusions that looked like small towers.

The whole chamber was warm and moist, as though they were inside the belly of a whale. Modo looked at the lit windows of the passenger railcar. If Octavia was anywhere, she was there.

No time like the present. Modo dropped down onto the ground. *Good!* No one had seen him.

He caught a flash of movement and turned. A hound leapt at him out of the shadows, jaws open.

CHAPTER 29

The Crick Crack Is the Best Way

"Are you alone?" The red-haired woman stood inside the passenger car, holding a glass of wine in her metal hand.

Octavia tried to give her a nasty look, but it was made difficult by the way the man holding her had twisted her neck. She yanked her arm, testing his grip. Not much chance of breaking free.

"I'm not alone," Octavia said. "A whole regiment of marines is coming."

"Ah, you are young and full of spite. I remember those days."

There wasn't so much as a glimmer of kindness in her eyes, only determination. What had Modo said her name was? Hack. No, something Nordic, so it ended with *dottir*. Hakkandottir.

The woman went on: "A pity we don't have time for conversation. Who sent you here?"

"Queen Victoria," Octavia answered. "Got a messenger pigeon from her this morning."

Hakkandottir took another sip of wine, then squeezed the glass till it shattered. "Alan sent you, correct?"

"Alan?"

At that Hakkandottir laughed. "Forgive me, you don't know that Mr. Socrates' first name is Alan. The old spider is still hard to kill."

Octavia remained expressionless. *Did that mean he had survived the attack in the house?*

"He's desperate, sending a child to spy on us. His Association falters."

The door opened and Fuhr stepped in, joints hissing. A man with short grey hair and glasses entered with him. His withered right arm was strengthened by a series of metal rings that encased it. His tiny hand was enhanced by several large metal fingers, so it looked as though he were wearing an iron glove. The contraption hissed steam as he pointed at Octavia.

"She belongs to Socrates," he said. "Her name is Octavia Milkweed. She's a very low cog in his network."

"Thank you for your unsolicited opinion," Hakkandottir said.

Octavia never forgot a face, and she had seen this one with Mr. Socrates several months ago. He was a member of the Permanent Association, but at that time his withered arm had no fancy attachments. "Gibbons," she said, for she rarely forgot a name either. "Named after the ape, I assume. Is your new hand especially designed to stab people in the back?"

"You witch!" he spat.

Hakkandottir smiled. "She is a clever little serpent, but ignore her. We have more pressing concerns. Do you have news, Fuhr?"

"Construction is complete. I must take the helm."

"Then do so. When our work is finished you will dump the instrument in the Thames. We do not want them to have our wondrous creation—is that understood?"

Fuhr nodded and said, "Understood perfectly, but understand this: don't be late collecting me. I'm not much of a swimmer any more."

"I'll be punctual, I promise. I'll summon the *Vesuvius* now to ensure my arrival. Gibbons, go to the observational platform. You won't want to miss the show."

When the two men had left, Hakkandottir moved to a table in the corner. On it was a collection of peculiar objects: pieces of clockwork, a phonograph, darkened eye goggles, a telegraph machine. With her metal fingers, she tapped out a message on the telegraph. Octavia couldn't see any wires, so she assumed it was wireless. She knew Mr. Socrates owned a similar device.

"Would you care to let me in on your plans?" she asked, trying to shake the henchman off again.

"We are about to strike a blow that will bring Britannia to her knees."

"How exciting."

"You mock me, child. Our interview is done." Hakkandottir clicked her fingers together, saying to her accomplice, "Kill her. Don't leave a mess." She met Octavia's eyes as she slipped on a long overcoat and left.

The man tightened his grip on her arms.

"You don't really want to murder me," she said.

The man jerked her forward a few steps. "I'm sorry, miss." His breath smelled like rotten sardines. "Orders is orders. Any other day I'd just give you an 'ow do ya do."

"Let's pretend today is one of those days."

He chuckled gruffly. "It don't work that way, miss. Now, I'm not one of them brutal types; I'm not wanting you to feel the pain. You got any partic'lar way you prefer? Smothering leaves a lovely corpse. Or how about a quick crick of the neck?"

"How about old age?"

He laughed again. "You're a brave one, and I admire that, miss, but I think the *crick crack* is best for both of us."

She tried to elbow him in the stomach but he squeezed her arm even tighter.

"Now, now."

When he released one arm to get a better hold on her shoulders, she slumped down. She pretended to weep, hoping for an ounce of pity in his heart. It seemed to only encourage him to hurry.

"I'll be quick, miss, I promise." He moved his hand to her neck. "Me father taught me this. On chickens, of course, 'e weren't no murderous sort, but the principle's the same."

He now had a tight hold on her head, but her left hand was free. She snaked it into the opening in her dress, feeling about for the stiletto. Finding the handle, she pulled it out and made to stab him in the leg, but he caught her hand and twisted it so hard she let out a cry. The stiletto clattered to the floor.

"You're a quick one! Can't blame you for trying."

Something boomed outside like a shell exploding, rattling the windows of the train car. "I'd better put the speed on or I'll miss the show. They promised it'd be a big one," the man said.

Octavia pulled and kicked and tried to bite him. "Best if you don't fight. It'll all be over in—"

The door banged open, striking the wall. Fuhr, sweaty and pale, stumbled in. He was dishevelled, his clothes covered with a cloak, and he had lost half his hair. He jerked his head but his gaze didn't focus on anything. In fact, to Octavia he looked blind. Then his eyes seemed to focus and he fell to his knees.

"Trouble," he moaned, "trouble out there."

"What is it, sir?"

"The gas. Exploded. The experiment. Failed." He put his hands on the desk and crawled to his feet, his sides heaving. Blotches scarred his face, as though he'd been splashed by acid. He staggered closer to them, gloved hands squeezed into fists. She heard a smack and a groan. Her captor fell back.

"Wot's that for, sir?" he cried, dropping Octavia.

When she tried to get up, the man kicked her in the stomach. She curled into a ball and looked up to see Fuhr knocking the man's head back. He smacked him a third time, straight on the jaw. The man fell, cracking his head on the desk on the way to the floor, where he lay in a heap.

Octavia got to her knees, holding her stomach. Fuhr's face seemed to be bubbling. He lurched forward as though he were about to fall on her. Where, where was the stiletto? There!

"Stay back!" she hissed as she snatched it from the floor and pointed it at him.

He blinked and staggered back, found his balance. "Octavia," he said in a familiar voice, "it's me. Modo. I . . . I'm here to save you."

CHAPTER 30

The Wicker Man

"Modo?"

To his relief, Octavia's look of horror turned to one of stark confusion. "But your face! You looked *just* like Fuhr."

He turned away, fumbled for his mask and shoved it back into place, quickly tightening the ties. "A mere trick: a sleight of face, instead of hands."

"It was more than that."

He rubbed the mutton chops from his face and showed them to her. "Dog hair. From a hound. I fought one of those beasts off just now. It nearly devoured my arm." He displayed his torn sleeve, stained with patches of his blood. "I shoved a steel bar in its mouth."

She was still gazing doubtfully at him when another loud *bang* shook the train car, followed by an engine coming to life. "Later, you'll have to explain that little face trick," she said, a hard edge to her voice. "You're keeping a secret from me. But we better see what's happening out there."

Modo pushed the door open a few inches and they could see men backing away from something that moved noisily inside the swirling smoke and steam. Hakkandottir, Hyde and another man observed from a scaffold ten feet above the action. The second man turned.

"That's Mr. Gibbons!" Modo said.

"Yes. And he has a brand-new mechanized arm."

"So *he* betrayed Mr. Socrates." Modo clenched his fists.

"There's not much we can do about that right now. What are they waiting for?"

At that moment, Fuhr rose up out of the great cloud of steam, standing on a footplate harnessed upright to a protective steel shield that curved around his back. He puffed on a cigar and manipulated a number of large levers. Two metal arms with pincers for fingers swung into the air, grabbed onto the edge of the cavern and pulled the rest of the machine higher. Each arm was constructed of rectangular metal boxes and inside each box a child was bolted. The machine swayed from side to side, metal screeching as it rose, revealing more of its torso and then Fuhr pulled back on the levers and a giant foot pressed onto the rocky floor. The machine stood at its full height.

Modo gaped at the sickening sight. It was fully fifty feet high and looked like the skeleton of a human body, with Fuhr at the head in his compartment. There were even glowing filaments running like veins throughout the appendages and rib cage and up the spine of the structure. The shoulder bolts held the children tightly in their metal frames.

Each time Fuhr jerked on a lever, the children crouched, pushed and straightened their backs as one to make the giant move. Modo estimated that at least a hundred children powered the machine. It boggled his mind to think they could be strong enough, even collectively and in their altered forms, to move all that iron.

"Is Oppie trapped in there?" Modo couldn't even begin to comprehend the boy's terror.

"I imagine so. Along with Ester. It's the most wretched thing I've ever seen," Octavia said.

Fuhr made the arms swing up and down. Two metal claws, the hands, opened and closed. The giant lumbered forward.

"It's a wicker man," Modo exclaimed.

"A what?"

"I saw an illustration—a giant wicker man that the Gauls would use as a cage for human sacrifices. They'd burn the people inside." He stared at the machine. "You know that schematic I stole from the Balcombe Street house . . . We thought it was a suit of armour. We just didn't have the right dimensions."

Workers were shining lights on the machine, revealing a larger square at the heart of it. The groaning figure inside the square was not a child, but a young man.

"That must be Prince Albert!" Modo said.

"You're right. The Prince at the heart of a horrible machine. This Clockwork Guild certainly loves its symbols. The papers will have a heyday!"

Dr. Hyde staggered up to the giant in awe, his arms raised as though he wanted to embrace it. His face had a look of absolute joy. "Dr. Hyde!" Hakkandottir shouted through a speaking trumpet. "Step back! We have to complete our tests!" But he still walked about, reaching to touch the metal ankles of the machine, hugging its calves. "Cornelius! Come back to me." He snapped out of his trance and climbed up to the platform, stealing another glance over his shoulder and shaking his head in wonder.

"Well, that was odd," Octavia said. "I just don't understand what this machine is meant for."

"I . . . I don't know. And how do they intend to get it out of here?"

Fuhr continued to pull the levers, grinning. One gigantic arm reached out and the pincers lifted a barrel and squeezed until it snapped in two, spraying water across the ground. The giant's arms swung about, knocking half the scaffolding over. Workers scattered and Fuhr let out a barking laugh.

Hakkandottir raised her speaking trumpet again. "The system is functioning properly. You may proceed, Mr. Fuhr!"

With that, Fuhr manipulated the levers so that both of the giant's arms were bent as though it were flexing its muscles. The ceiling was only a few feet above it now. The left arm shot straight up, driving the pincers directly into the rock, which cracked. The right arm followed, then both arms struck again and again, causing dirt and shattered stones to rain down. A beam of sunlight shot through the cavern's ceiling, illuminating the giant's gleaming arms.

When the opening was large enough Fuhr shouted, "For the Clockwork Guild!"

The giant grabbed on to something outside with its claws and began a slow, deliberate climb out of the cavern and into the streets of London.

CHAPTER 31

A Stroll Through London Town

Modo and Octavia watched as the giant pulled its iron foot through the hole and disappeared. It was as if the thing had never existed; as though they'd imagined it all.

Octavia put her hand to her mouth. "I never dreamed I'd ever see anything . . ." She tightened her grip on Modo's shoulder. "We must stop it, of course, but I haven't the faintest . . ."

"We could go back down the tunnel the way we came and take a cab to . . ." He paused. His mind wasn't working properly. It would take too long to travel that far. "Never mind."

She pointed at the hole in the roof of the cavern. "That's the quickest way out."

Modo nodded. "It'll take some doing."

Scaffolding at least six storeys high stood somewhat shakily below the opening. They'd have to risk their necks, but the top of the scaffolding looked close enough for them to leap up and grab the lip of the hole.

Modo heard a *pop* and ducked, pulling Octavia down with him. They peeked through the door again in time to see Gibbons holding up a fizzing champagne bottle and splashing its contents into glasses. Several of the men in greatcoats and Hakkandottir poured the drink and clinked glasses.

"Let's leave them to their celebration," Octavia said.

They stole out of the train car, edged along the wall to the corner of the scaffolding and began climbing. Modo was impressed that Octavia was able to match his speed. Soon they were clinging to the thin metal bars three-quarters of the way up.

He kept an eye on the people below. Hyde was still staring at the open hole looking pleased. Hakkandottir shouted orders, while her men set dynamite among the machines used to create the giant.

Then, as though she had felt his eyes on her, she looked up directly at Modo and shouted. Two men fired pistols; bullets zinged off the wall behind them.

"Faster!" Octavia hissed. "Climb!"

They scrambled higher and higher. They hoped the coal smoke and steam hanging in the air would help to hide them.

The guns had stopped firing and Modo paused to see why. Octavia kept climbing. Modo could just make out Hakkandottir and Dr. Hyde walking towards the train car. She put her metal hand on Hyde's shoulder. The possibility that she was being affectionate towards him made Modo feel sick.

It occurred to him that they could set dynamite under the scaffolding's supports, and just then he felt the scaffolding shaking and looked down. A shape lunged out of the mist below.

"You won't tell anyone about this!" Gibbons said, using his powerful new arm to launch himself the last few yards and latch onto Modo's ankle.

His metal fingers squeezed so hard that Modo let out a yell.

"Traitor!" Modo shouted, trying to shake him off.

"Just a matter of shifting perspectives!" Gibbons spat out.

His eyes blazed behind his fogged glasses. He pulled so hard that Modo nearly lost his grip. They were both going to fall.

"Kick him in the head," Octavia yelled from above.

Modo feinted a kick at Gibbons's head, then stomped on the man's support hand. Gibbons let go of the scaffolding, but kept a tight hold on Modo, clutching both his legs.

Modo remembered Mr. Socrates' belt pouch and drew out the first thing he could put his fingers on. He pointed it at Gibbons, realizing too late that it was the fountain pen.

Gibbons paused to look at it and was just about to laugh, when Modo pressed the button and black ink shot out, staining Gibbons's face. His skin began to sizzle. He screamed, clutching his eyes as he fell to the ground.

Modo, frightened of what was still dripping from the pen, dropped it and climbed up to Octavia.

"Next time kick him in the head," she said.

At the top of the scaffolding, Modo was heartened by the late afternoon sunlight.

"Stand still!" Octavia grabbed his shoulders. "I'll use you as a ladder."

He put out his hand and supported her weight, his legs shaking, the wood slats of the scaffold creaking. She stepped directly on his shoulder, then leapt onto the stone ledge above them.

Modo jumped up and grabbed the ledge, while Octavia knelt and took his other dirty, gloved hand. She heaved and pulled until his chest hung over the lip of the hole. Kicking and squirming he wriggled the rest of the way onto the ground, and when he'd finally caught his breath, he stood up.

St. James Square! He'd spent hours perched atop the London Library, looking down at the peaceful garden. Now, the statue of William III on his horse had been swatted aside; the iron fence surrounding it had been flattened. A woman with a baby stroller was still cowering with fear behind a bench. Water streamed in an arc where the giant had broken a fountain in two. A tree, its roots covered in dirt, lay tossed across a bench. On the southern edge of the road a Hansom cab had been overturned. One horse was still standing, the other on its side, kicking. A man's legs stuck out from under the cab.

"We must keep moving," Octavia said, hiking up the front of her skirts and tucking them into her sash. The pantaloons looked more like britches. "I'll be faster now."

"We can't go yet," Modo said. He darted over to the Hansom cab, Octavia at his heels. Another man joined him; they grabbed the axle and lifted. Modo grunted, straining every muscle, raising the cab an inch, then another. People stopped to watch. "Pull," he barked. "Pull the driver out!"

Octavia dragged the driver to safety. His shins were bent back at an awkward angle and he groaned, "Me gams! Me gams!" Modo dropped the cab, only realizing then that it was a bobby who had helped him with the lifting.

"What strength! Good work!" The police constable tipped his canvas hat back. He looked Modo up and down. "Why are you wearing a mask?"

"A boiler accident."

"You've been beaten all to pieces. You came out of that hole. What's happening down there?"

Octavia grabbed Modo's hand. "I'm sorry, sir, but I must get my brother to the hospital."

As they ran across the square they heard him shout, "Halt! I want to speak with you!"

They sped straight out the south end of the square and careened onto Pall Mall, passing the Travellers Club and Norfolk House. It was easy to tell where the giant had been; wagons were overturned and people stared in horror in the direction it had gone. Modo and Octavia dodged through clusters of people, skirting halted omnibuses. Two men with sandwich boards displaying PATENT BOOT BLACK shrank back against the door to Queens Theatre.

"Where's he steering that thing?" Octavia huffed as they ran.

"The shipyard?" Modo could picture the giant poking holes in the sides of ships. But if the Guild wanted to sink ships, dynamite would be a much simpler weapon.

Partway down Pall Mall another statue lay on the ground shattered. Soon, Modo saw the giant slouching towards Trafalgar Square, coaches and carts scattering before it. With one arm the giant pushed over an omnibus, the horses neighing and breaking out of their harnesses, the passengers inside screaming, the ones topside leaping to the ground. The giant plowed through the busy square, stepping past a bronze lion and smacking a claw against Nelson's Column, chipping the granite. Modo expected the statue of Nelson to tumble to the ground, but it stood firm. The giant stepped into a fountain and out again, turning as though it had just made up its mind to visit the National Gallery but then staggered in the opposite direction.

Fuhr's lost! Modo thought. It began to move clumsily down Charing Cross Road, the paving stones shattering like glass under its metal feet.

Modo and Octavia ran as fast as they could, but the giant was picking up speed. Its gait was no longer so lopsided. Fuhr was gaining confidence in its operation.

"The Houses of Parliament!" Octavia exclaimed.

"Of course," Modo replied. If only he could climb to the rooftops, he'd move so much faster, but he could never abandon Octavia. He pushed past a stunned gentleman leaning on an umbrella and slipped between two barristers in white wigs. He briefly lost sight of the giant, then the crowds grew more sparse and he and Octavia were able to run again, heading for the Houses of Parliament.

They heard gunfire as the monstrous machine lumbered across the green lawn towards Parliament. The four guards fired away; gun muzzles flashing.

Modo thought: *No! Don't hit the children!*

He and Octavia raced across the yard just as the machine took two quick strides and swatted away the guards.

Fuhr yanked on a lever and the giant's iron claw smashed

the second-storey windows of Parliament. Another lever made the giant kick down a door. Clerks streamed out like ants.

"How do we stop it?" Octavia shouted.

How? Modo still couldn't believe that something so horrendous existed.

There was a clattering behind them, and they turned to see a black carriage bounce off the road and onto the grass; the horses stopped just before trampling Modo. He backed away and stood next to Octavia. The driver was a soldier in an unfamiliar black uniform, a rifle in a holster beside him. He jumped down, straightened his jacket and opened the door to the carriage.

Holding on to a top hat, out stepped Mr. Socrates.

CHAPTER 32

Standing on the Shoulders of a Giant

"Ah, you *are* alive. Good," Mr. Socrates said, putting on his top hat. "A few of my other agents weren't so lucky." His left eye was bruised, and despite his jaunty manner he looked tired and somehow older. His suit needed pressing. Tharpa stood behind him, a neatly stitched slash now embellishing his jawline.

"So, Modo, what exactly is the contraption?" Mr. Socrates asked.

Modo wanted to grab Mr. Socrates and hug him. But he had enough control not to blurt out his joy. "Mr. Socrates . . . your eye. What . . . ?"

"It's none of your concern, Modo," he snapped. "I asked you a question."

"Yes, sir," he answered, forcing himself to concentrate. "We saw it being built in a chamber below Saint James

Square. The missing orphans power it somehow. Fuhr is in control of it."

Mr. Socrates watched calmly as the giant continued to smash its claw into the second-storey windows of Westminster Hall and dragged out a hapless occupant.

"Impressive," he said. "The Guild engineered this right under our noses. I'd thought the young men who attacked their parents were the real threat, but no, they were merely a decoy, throwing us off the track of the larger plan. This machine is . . . well . . . beyond all imagination."

"Prince Albert is part of the machine," Octavia said.

"He is?" Mr. Socrates reached into his greatcoat, took out a small telescope and looked through it. "I see. That complicates things. And Miss Hakkandottir?"

"Underground," Octavia said. "She said they'll sink the machine in the Thames when they're done."

"That's not good news."

"Not good news?" Octavia said. "*That's* a bloody understatement!"

"Watch your tongue, Miss Milkweed," Mr. Socrates said. "Even in times of crisis it's important you maintain your composure."

"My composure is fine, thank you very much, considering what has been done to so many orphans!"

Modo became distracted from their quarrel by a niggling thought. There was something about the giant he just couldn't put his finger on. It was made of tons of iron, sheet metal, gears. But even with so many children built into the body of the machine, it was impossible that they could bear the weight of all of that and keep the giant standing upright for so long. Something else was at play. But what?

A team of muscular brown horses pulled a large, steel-plated carriage across the Old Palace Yard. It stopped at Mr. Socrates' signal. "I received a telegram informing me there was an event down here," Mr. Socrates said. "I brought reinforcements." The doors opened and soldiers in black uniforms climbed out, carrying rifles. Three unhooked a small field gun from the back of the carriage.

"In a few minutes our problems will be solved," Mr. Socrates said.

"But what about the children?" Octavia asked incredulously.

A flash of concern crossed Mr. Socrates' face. "We will do our best to prevent unnecessary deaths. It is all we can do." He turned towards an officer. "When you have your weapon set up, fire. Begin by aiming at its head, at the man who's controlling the machine. Do what you can to avoid the children, and most especially the young man at the centre of the giant. You won't want to kill Prince Albert."

The officer went pale. "Prince Albert, sir?"

"Good, you were listening. So aim well."

The officer saluted and marched back to his men.

"There must be a better way," Modo said. What if Oppie were struck by a shell? "You can't fire at it."

"People are dying as we speak," Mr. Socrates said. "Important people. You have to make hard choices in this business. We can only do our best."

At that moment, the field gun's boom nearly deafened Modo. The shell struck the metal shield behind Fuhr and exploded, clouding the shoulders of the giant with smoke.

"Excellent shot!" Mr. Socrates shouted, but when the smoke cleared they could see that Fuhr was unharmed. As though the shell had been little more than a pesky fly, he continued to bash at another part of the building.

"We'll have to try another approach," Mr. Socrates said.

Modo continued to wrestle with the notion that the machine worked at all. He felt in his coat pocket and pulled out the torn piece of paper that had Hyde's notations. He skimmed it, and two lines jumped out at him.

harnesses the inner potency! This is the discovery! it

this energy can be directed through a filament to gyro

There were filaments all along the giant, glowing with light; some kind of energy was lighting them. Not electricity, so the source had to be on the giant. The filaments were attached to the children. Gyroscopes were spinning, proving that there was an energy source: *harnesses the inner potency.*

"Could it be," said Modo, "that Dr. Hyde has discovered an energy inside the children that powers the giant?" He held the paper up to Mr. Socrates. "Look! We found a portion of Dr. Hyde's notes in their experimental chamber."

Mr. Socrates took the scrap, sniffed at the scent of sewer that still clung to it, then examined it. "This is unreadable. I can't make a decision based on a fragment of incoherent handwriting and a guess."

"But, sir, I'm certain that I'm correct."

"Even if you were, Modo, what difference could it make

now?" He turned away. "Men! Load! Aim for the legs!"

"Nooo!" Modo pulled on Mr. Socrates' arm and for an angry moment he felt as though he were that child in Ravenscroft again.

Mr. Socrates jerked his arm out of Modo's grip. "You've done your part. We'll handle everything from here."

Modo took a step back, dejected. He watched all the children moving as one. He thought of Oppie and how the boy had delivered him his food, taken care of him. There were a hundred Oppies in there. They didn't deserve this. There had to be a better way.

He studied Mr. Socrates as he marched about, giving more orders. *He doesn't see the children*, Modo thought. *Doesn't know them or their lives. He was never poor.* Modo couldn't control himself any more; he began running with his telltale lope towards the giant.

"Hold fire!" Mr. Socrates shouted. "Modo, I order you to return!"

"Modo!" Octavia cried.

Her voice made him falter, but Modo charged on. He stormed across the grass, past the statue of Richard the Lionheart.

The giant had its back to him and Fuhr was busy driving it towards another pillar, which it smashed. More people were flushed from the building, while others looked out the windows unaware of the danger.

The children were still silent, pushing and pulling with their legs and spines, faces set in angry determination. The filaments running from their shoulder bolts glowed throughout the machine, sparks shooting. Their life energy, Modo was certain of it now.

Modo leapt at the metal ankle of the machine and latched on to it. The moment he touched the steel, the hair on his arms stood on end as though an electrical charge were going through him. He found himself face to face with a girl whose hair was askew, her eyes wide and her face deformed by the tincture. The bolts in her shoulders held her tight inside the frame. Filaments had been attached to each shoulder bolt. One glowed bright red, and the girl bent her legs at the same time as all the children in her row. As they lifted their legs, so too did the giant.

"I'll help you," Modo cried.

The girl made no response; her eyes were blank. He climbed up the calf. The machine hissed as it moved. If he could free them, one by one, surely that would stop the giant and Fuhr—but there were too many of them and he had no way of undoing the bolts.

His best hope was to stop Fuhr.

He climbed to the hips, then clambered over to the iron spine and headed up it, careful not to get his fingers crushed in the moving vertebrae. He imagined tomorrow's papers with drawings depicting England's own children destroying the heart of the Empire.

Fuhr smashed a gargoyle, taking out the wall behind it. Modo scrambled onto the shoulders, and found his balance on the small deck. Fuhr, with his back to Modo, focused on the guards who were firing at him. The giant reached down, swept them aside and lifted its leg to step on one.

Now that he was so close, what to do? Fuhr was belted in behind the levers, his back and head protected by the metal shell. Close up, Modo could see how much the head was like a giant helmet housing Fuhr's body. The man sucked on a cigar as if he were out on a stroll, the smoke drifting into the air. The arms of his suit had been torn, revealing his own metal limbs.

"Fuhr!" Octavia called.

She stood a few yards in front of the giant. "Fuhr! You're surrounded! Surrender now!"

Fuhr exhaled laughter and smoke. Then, to Modo's horror, he brought the giant's arm down towards her.

CHAPTER 33

Using the Gift

At the last moment Octavia dodged out of the way and the claws thudded into the ground, tearing up the grass. She took a moment to look right at Modo and he was certain it was an admonishing glance, then she dodged a second blow. She was trying to send a message to him, but what? He slapped the side of his head. Of course! She was providing a distraction.

Modo leapt from the shoulder to the head of the giant and slugged Fuhr in the jaw, knocking the cigar and a grunt out of his mouth. Fuhr lashed out at Modo, his hand clicking an inch from Modo's throat because the harness prevented him from reaching any farther. Modo dashed to the other side of Fuhr, struck another blow, then backed away.

"Who are you?" Fuhr shouted, pulling on a lever.

Modo had a sudden fearful thought: what if he knocked Fuhr unconscious? Would the machine collapse and crush the children? He heard something behind him, and turned just in time to be swatted into the air by the giant's hand. He landed at the far end of the shoulder deck, slipping off its edge. He hung there by his fingers until he found a place to dig in his toes so he could cling to the side of the shoulder. He was able to swing partway down the back, out of Fuhr's sight.

From there he had an excellent view of the filaments in the spine, and the energy that was flowing through them, making the machine walk and grasp. The wires seemed to glow more brightly than ever. But what was the true source?

He climbed down a bit lower, looking at the blank-eyed children. The tincture had changed them; their faces were set in cold anger. He thought of Oscar Featherstone and how Oscar had felt that the other side of him, the side that attacked his father, was full of rage. That anger was what connected these children.

Modo clambered over the ribs of the shuddering giant as it lurched left, right, left, right, like a drunken sailor. Its shoulders bumped Victoria Tower and it lumbered through trees, snapping off thick branches.

He examined the twisted wolflike faces of the children, their hate-filled, blank eyes. Maybe the anger was part of what powered them. And if it was, how could he stop it?

He had his own anger—he knew what it was like to be forsaken, forgotten. They had that in common. Always hungry, always wanting a warmer place to sleep. Somehow Dr. Hyde had opened the tap to this in each child. It became clear to him what he must do.

He swung down and stopped directly in front of a girl with blond hair, and hung there by one hand. With his other hand he removed his mask, revealing the full ugliness of his

face. The girl's eyes were blank, staring past him, and he
thought perhaps his intuition had been wrong.

"I understand," he said. "I know your anger. You don't
have to listen to the voices."

There was no reaction. Maybe the tincture's hold was too
strong to break. After all, it had forced Oscar to kill his own
father. No! There had to be a way. Modo reached a trembling hand and cupped the girl's cheek. "There are people
who care about you, who love you," he whispered. "I care
about you." The girl's face softened and she looked directly
at him and did not flinch at the sight of his face. She let out
a sigh and stopped moving her legs up and down, stopped
powering her section of the machine. The filaments around
her grew dull and the gyroscope slowed to a standstill.

Modo moved over to the next child, a boy, and looked
right into his brown eyes. "I understand you. Your anger.
Listen to your own voice." This time it happened more
quickly. The boy looked, he saw, he understood and slowed
his movements.

"I understand," Modo said, crawling from child to child.
Each one looked at his face and didn't shudder. He smiled
at every one. "There is a better way." They began to whisper to one another as though passing on a long-forgotten
secret. The whispers grew to a chattering. Soon the giant's
legs slowed and stopped. More and more children began to
babble. The machine stood still.

But Modo had brought the giant to a stop only a few feet
past Parliament and teetering on the edge of the Thames. If
it fell, all the children would drown.

Fuhr was shouting from above.

Modo put his mask back on and climbed up. Fuhr was out of his harness, running around the shoulder deck yelling at the children. Then he pulled on the levers. "Move! Move!"

Bullets ricocheted off the metal plates of the giant. Modo turned, intending to shout at the soldiers to stop, but none of them were firing. There was a droning in the distance. The bullets seemed to be coming out of the very air itself. Modo dashed across the deck to give Fuhr a push, but the man whipped around.

"You! You're Modo! Gibbons told us about an agent who wore a mask. I've torn bigger men in two."

In one leap Fuhr was next to Modo, unleashing a steam-powered punch that smashed his mask to pieces and knocked him to the edge of the giant's shoulder. Modo threw a hand up to his cheek, feeling as though his jaw was broken. His face! It was exposed to Fuhr, to the world. He thought of leaping across to Parliament and escaping, but instead rose to his feet and turned to his enemy.

When Fuhr got his first clear look at Modo's face, he hesitated. "Are you the Devil?" he asked. "No, you can't be. Not even the Devil could be so ugly."

Modo had expected him to be cruel, but his words still cut deep into him.

The thrumming was closer now, and behind Fuhr, Modo could see a conical grey airship drifting out of the fog. Steel plating protected the front and a large rotor powered it. Hakkandottir was in the carriage brandishing a rifle. Three men stood around her, including Dr. Hyde, who gazed sadly at the giant. Beside him a man wearing goggles lowered a rope ladder.

"Jump, Mr. Fuhr! Jump!" he hollered.

"I'll track you down, devil-boy," Fuhr said, giving him a sideways look. "And I'll throttle you until your ugly face turns blue. That's my promise." He leapt, grabbing on to the dangling ladder.

Hakkandottir fired at Modo, almost hitting him. He was still so angry at Fuhr, at all of them for what they had done to the children, that he bounded to the edge of the giant, jumped and latched onto Fuhr's leg. The airship drew away, taking them over the Thames. Fuhr kicked at him but Modo tightened his grip.

"You won't escape!" he cried.

Hakkandottir aimed her rifle, shouting, "Get out of the way, Fuhr. I need a clear shot."

Fuhr reached down to pry Modo off his leg, but just then one side of the rope ladder snapped and they swung outwards, dangling by the remaining half.

Fuhr growled and tried to climb higher, but the rest of the rope broke. Fuhr's hands found Modo's throat as they tumbled through the sky and into the Thames.

CHAPTER 34

The Thames

As they hit the water, Fuhr's hold was too strong for Modo to break. Modo had been prevented from sucking in a final gasp of air, and now they were sinking into the murky, cold water. All Modo could see was his enemy's angry face. Fuhr's was a two-handed death grip. They would both be dragged to the bottom, thanks to his metal appendages. Modo pounded against the man's enormous chest. They sank deeper and deeper, until Modo felt his lungs would explode.

Fuhr's arm bubbled, his grasp suddenly loosening and his one arm falling uselessly to his side.

Modo brought his legs up against Fuhr's lower stomach. Fuhr's lips were moving and his hold on Modo's throat grew even tighter. Modo gave him a two-footed kick, broke his grip and flailed away. Fuhr lunged at Modo, but he sank heavily into the depths.

Modo's lungs demanded air. He kicked, his frenzied thrashing taking him in circles. A realization burned: *If I*

*hadn't been trapped inside Ravenscroft for my entire child-
hood, I'd bloody well know how to swim.*

Tharpa's voice came to him then, as though he were speaking directly into his ear: *No matter the situation, be calm.*
Modo stopped his thrashing and allowed himself to drift. He
let out the tiniest bubble and noted which direction it went.
Up! That way is up! He kicked with purpose now. The surface was far above him, but the light was getting closer.

He kicked and kicked. *Mrs. Finchley!* he thought. *Octavia!* He churned his limbs, trying to reach the world above
him, but he had used the last of his reserves. He couldn't
stop from gulping in a mouthful of the putrid Thames. And
another. He gulped until his lungs were full, and he sank.

CHAPTER 35

Into the Murk

Octavia had followed the airship on foot up to the top of the river wall, right next to Parliament. The moment Modo fell from the sky, she yanked off her dress and dove into the Thames. She swam to a cluster of bubbles, then shot straight down, her eyes open and stinging in the dirty water. She spotted more bubbles and followed them down, down, until she felt she could go no farther. She scissor-kicked to the surface, gasped in a deep breath and dove again. The gloomy water gave up no sign of Modo. She began to feel sick to her stomach.

She searched the water for more bubbles, and saw none, so she kicked into the depths then back up for another gulp of air and straight down again.

She'd spent months training alongside Tharpa, including learning to swim. *Control your breath*, he'd told her. *Let it out slowly and you'll go deeper*. She did this now, kicking and kicking to the bottom of the river. After what felt like hours she finally saw a form nearby, and propelled herself towards it. The pressure hurt her ears. She grabbed at the ragged shape. It had arms and legs, but it was too dark to see it. She pulled and strained every muscle in her body as she swam up, dragging the form with her.

She broke the surface and inhaled madly, then looked at the body in her hands and caught a glimpse of ragged red hair. Modo? Her eyes stung with the filthy water, her vision blurred, so his face appeared twisted and grotesque. The world was silent—all she heard was her heartbeat.

Her feet found purchase on the riverbank and she dragged him to the wharf. A pair of hands lifted Modo from her arms and she looked up to see Tharpa.

"Do you need aid?" he said.

She shook her head, trembling uncontrollably. He carried Modo a few feet away.

Octavia climbed onto the wharf, coughing, her hair plastered over her eyes so she got only a glimpse of Modo. She got the impression of a jutting lip, a bloated cheek, a drooping eye. She wiped away the foul water with her fingers, believing there was something wrong with her eyes. Tharpa was pushing down on Modo's chest and stomach with tremendous force. When he saw Octavia watching, he shifted position, blocking her view of Modo.

She coughed and belched water, then fell back on the hard planks of the dock, closing her eyes. A soldier brought her a blanket and said something, but her ears were still blocked. She'd swallowed half the Thames. All that disgusting water was inside her. Lying on her side, Octavia spat out whatever she could bring up. Then two shiny military riding boots stepped into her line of vision. It took her a moment to realize they were filled by someone.

"You did well." Mr. Socrates sounded as though he were talking from the far end of a tunnel. "Octavia. You are a perfect angel."

"Angel?" Her voice was ragged. Her ears popped painfully and the noise of the world rushed in.

"Agent," Mr. Socrates corrected. "We don't need angels here." And with that he laughed.

"He lives!" Tharpa shouted. "He draws breath!"

"Thank you," Octavia said to no one in particular, and heaved a great sigh of relief.

CHAPTER 36

The Dying Fires

Fuhr sank upright, his feet landing firmly on the bottom of the Thames. His lungs yearned for air. He was too heavy to swim, but he lifted his legs and pushed forward, finding solid rocks buried in the silt. He took another step and another. A shell hadn't killed him; bullets hadn't killed him; some ugly devil-child wouldn't be his end.

He saw the posts of a dock only twenty yards away and he slouched towards them. He would climb the dock and finish destroying his enemy and anyone else who stood in his way. Twenty long steps. He could make it.

Water seeped into the coal chamber in his right leg, and the limb bubbled to a stop. He lifted his left leg, but slipped, and was forced to crawl on the bottom of the river, using only one arm and one leg. He was fifteen yards away. Fourteen. He would climb the dock and strangle the boy.

The chamber in his left leg died. He dragged himself with one hand, digging deep into the riverbed, an inch at a time.

The coal fire sputtered and died in that arm too. He was motionless. He wanted to scream in anger.

He had to breathe. He couldn't wait another second.

All that surrounded him was water.

CHAPTER 37

A Marvel and a Monstrosity

Modo sputtered and gagged and drew in several gasping breaths. He gradually became aware that his head rested on hard planks and a dull light was shining in his eyes. It was the sun, shrouded by fog. A moment later it was blotted out by a dark shape. He blinked and saw that Tharpa was floating there, his lips moving silently. Modo's ears crackled and he heard the words "Young sahib, are you well?"

Modo nodded slowly and let out another wet cough. His hand went to his face, and Tharpa handed him a scarf, which Modo pulled up to his nose. With Tharpa's help, he slowly sat up. It took him another few minutes before he muttered, "Must stand."

Tharpa helped him to his feet and allowed Modo to lean on him. The scene around them came into focus. They were at the wharf near Parliament, Victoria Tower casting a long shadow. A line of soldiers in crimson coats had set up barricades at the west end of the park to keep the curious away. It all seemed so oddly ordinary to Modo, as though he saw this sort of thing every day.

The giant stood at the edge of the Houses of Parliament, right next to the Thames, as if it had been there for a hundred years, frozen in position with one metallic arm hanging at its side. The other arm was caught in the topmost branches of a tree.

Soldiers in black uniforms climbed wooden ladders, working with wrenches and saws to release the children, many of whom already lay on the ground, or sat, leaning against one another. Other soldiers had begun to dismantle the top of the giant's frame, loading the pieces onto wagons and driving them to the wharf, where they were being loaded onto a barge. The Prince was already gone; Modo assumed he had been the first to be rescued.

Mr. Socrates stood near the giant, leaning on his walking stick. Occasionally, those officers in black uniforms would come up to receive commands from him, then march double-time to their tasks.

Modo walked haltingly towards the children, each step a labour. A cherub-faced soldier was giving pieces of chocolate to the ones who were awake. Others appeared to be asleep. Modo had expected that a few of them would be dead and was glad, so glad, to not see any who had perished. Finally, he found the one he was looking for.

"Oppie," he said.

The boy looked up. He was holding a chocolate bar, his fingers sticky. "Wot?" he said.

His face still looked puffy, his body enlarged by the tincture, but Modo could see some of the boy's finer features coming back.

"I'm Mr. Wellington," Modo said.

"Oh, it's Mr. W, is it? You're here too. Fancy 'at."

"I was investigating all of this. And I'm so glad you weren't harmed," Modo said.

"'Armed? Well, me too, guvnuh," he said, taking another bite of chocolate.

Modo noticed a military cross pinned to his shirt. "Where did you get that?"

"Prince Albert gave me that just before they took him away. Said 'e's going to give me a tour of Buckin'am."

Modo grinned. "I hope you'll still have time to listen to the rest of *Varney*."

"Will I! You bet, Mr. W."

"Well, I'll look you up in the next while. And we can do that."

Modo stepped back a few feet. The boy continued eating and Modo watched with satisfaction. Oppie was alive. He looked around at the other children and spotted a girl with red hair gulping down her own chocolate. Could she be Ester? They were all alive, coming back to their old selves.

At his back he heard a step and a small *thud*. Without turning Modo said, "Mr. Socrates, I presume."

Mr. Socrates laughed. "Welcome back to the land of the living. You accomplished an impressive feat. You must feel proud."

Modo felt only bone-weary. "Thank you."

"That structure . . . It really was a marvel. We have much to learn from it."

"It was a monstrosity."

"You are mistaken, Modo. What Dr. Hyde and the Clock-work Guild did to the children was immoral. The young should not be used to fight battles; that's not the gentleman's way. But the war machine itself is a marvel of scientific inge-nuity. Imagine twenty of them on a battlefield."

Modo wanted to disagree, but thought better of it. "Why did the Guild do it?" he asked. "What did they hope to gain?"

"It's a symbolic first strike. My best guess is that they hoped that papers all across the world would report on this incident. We'll cover up what details we can, but we cannot hide the fact that the Houses of Parliament, the very heart of our Empire, were attacked. What they want to spread is fear. Sometimes governments are paralyzed just waiting for the next blow. They begin pointing fingers at one another, markets falter, and soon the peasants are out in the streets sharpening their axes. But you shouldn't trouble yourself thinking about all this business now. You need some rest."

"Gibbons—that is, *Mr.* Gibbons, he . . ." Modo's breath was laboured. ". . . betrayed you."

Mr. Socrates gave Modo a sharp look. "Explain."

"I had a run-in with him in the chamber under St. James Square. With Miss Hakkandottir."

Mr. Socrates patted Modo's shoulder. "That is important information. Thank you. I'll have Tharpa take you to a safe place to recover from this assignment." He paused. "I'm very pleased with what you've done in these last few days."

Modo nodded. "It was only my duty, sir."

Mr. Socrates smiled. "Yes. Duty. If only we all felt as much loyalty to it as you do."

As Tharpa guided him into the carriage, Modo asked, "Where's Octavia?"

"She has returned to the Langham. She was tired and wet."

"Wet?"

"She's the one who pulled you out of the river."

"She did?" He remembered seeing her swim towards him. He'd thought it was an angel. He'd believed he was dead.

"Then," he said in amazement, "I owe her my life."

"Yes," Tharpa said, as he sat in the seat across from Modo. He banged on the roof, and with the clomping of hooves, the carriage rolled down Abingdon Street, leaving the giant, the children, the soldiers and the smashed Houses of Parliament behind.

CHAPTER 38

Behind the Mask

On his fourth day of rest Modo sat on a chaise longue at the edge of a large balcony overlooking Kew Gardens. The view of shrubs, trees and a glass house reminded him of Ravenscroft. He passed his time dressed in nightclothes and a heavy, warm robe, his face hidden behind a white mask. A nightcap hid his pockmarked skull. The sun warmed him, and a pug-nosed servant brought him tea and food and the *Times* whenever he desired it. He was becoming especially fond of croissants and jam.

Not once did he see a mention in the papers of the attack on the Houses of Parliament. All he found were a couple of paragraphs about renovations and a piece about a tunnel collapsing directly beneath St. James Square. Obviously the Permanent Association's influence ran deep within the publishers' networks. How all the witnesses were silenced, Modo didn't know. But if no one would print their words other than the most disreputable papers, the whole event eventually would become little more than fodder for drunken pub tales.

Today Modo's morning paper ritual was interrupted by the tap of a walking stick and the scrape of a chair on the floor. He lowered the *Times* to see Mr. Socrates sitting across from him. The bruise below his eye was gone.

"How goes your recuperation?" he asked.

"I'm doing well, sir. I enjoy being pampered."

"You deserve the rest. You achieved so much in a short time."

Modo smiled behind the mask. "I've been taught well."

Mr. Socrates let out a short laugh. "I don't need compliments, young man. And let's not forget that you did disobey me when you chose to confront the mechanized leviathan on your own. I suppose it's a sign that you can think for yourself—but I could have lost you."

Was that emotion in his voice? Modo looked him in the eyes, but they gave nothing away.

"Don't disobey me again," Mr. Socrates said.

If I hadn't disobeyed you, many of those children would have died. Modo decided it was best just to nod in agreement.

"What will become of the orphans?" he asked, finally.

"They lost their wolflike features as the tincture wore off, and so far none of them has had any measurable after-effects. We've been removing the bolts so they can live normal lives. The Association has set up an orphanage for the ones who have no caregivers. In time they'll likely find employment in the Colonies."

"There was a boy, his name was Oppie—what of him?"

"Oppie? Yes, Octavia also asked about him. And about

the girl, Ester. Both my agents appear to have become a little too sentimental." But he said this with a smile. "Oppie is healing and will soon be delivered to his parents. He seems to have suffered no ill effects. But only time will tell."

"That's good news then." Modo sipped his tea. "And what of Gibbons?"

Mr. Socrates shrugged. "He was found in the Thames, a knife in his back. I assume the Clockwork Guild was finished with him."

Modo couldn't help but wonder if Mr. Socrates was telling the truth. Gibbons had, after all, been a double agent. It was best not to dwell on it. He buttered a croissant, watching as two swans landed in a pond in the distant gardens.

"I do worry about Oscar Featherstone," Modo said.

"Ah, that is an unfortunate situation. He will be hanged next week."

"But he's innocent!"

"No one outside our circle knows about Hyde's tincture, so his lawyer cannot use it for his defence. Oscar did kill his father; there's no way to stop justice once its wheels have begun to roll."

"That's not fair!"

Mr. Socrates shook his head. "It's not about fairness, Modo. There are some things that cannot be revealed. It's that simple." He got up from his chair. "I want you to rest your mind and body. That's your assignment now. You're not to be concerned about the larger picture; all is unfolding as it should." He took a step to go, then turned back. "You have another visitor, by the way. I shall send her up."

Modo tapped his fingers together nervously. *Mrs. Finchley? Octavia?* He wasn't sure which one he wanted to see more. He didn't have time to change his face, but he made his body longer, his hump less obvious and his shoulders a little wider.

A minute later Octavia appeared on the balcony in a blue dress and a thick white shawl. The sight of her made him draw in a deep breath, and his nostrils whistled. Thankfully, she didn't seem to hear it. He wished he could take her for a walk in Kew Gardens.

"Miss Milkweed," he said.

"Mr. Modo."

"Apparently, I owe you my life."

"Yes," she said simply. "I'm not sure what overtook me."

"Perhaps you couldn't live without my sense of humour."

She laughed. "I see you are feeling better."

"Much better. Well-fed too. I'm as stuffed as a Christmas turkey."

"Good. Good."

She seemed distracted, not quite herself. Modo wasn't certain what to say, so he asked, "And how are you?"

"I am well."

A silence descended. She looked out over Kew Gardens and said, "It is a beautiful view."

"Especially now that you are here." He hadn't meant to say that out loud. Perhaps the drop of morphine he had taken had loosened his tongue.

Octavia gave him a crooked smile. "There are two things that confuse me, Modo. The first is about myself. I don't know why I dove into that water after you. It felt as though it was about more than just trying to save a comrade."

Modo wanted to say *Maybe you have feelings for me*, but he had already said something foolish enough. His heart was a hummingbird.

"As I said, it confuses me. Why would I risk my life? Do you have an answer?"

"Me?"

"Yes, you."

"I—I don't know," he said. He couldn't utter another word. She was so beautiful, he thought, and he remembered his own revulsion each time he looked in the mirror.

"I am also confused . . . about who you are, exactly. So far I have seen you with two faces, if that makes sense. It's impossible, but it was not my imagination. I'd like to know which one was real. I have to know what you look like. Then I will know who you are."

"I can't explain it," he said.

"Don't you trust me?"

"Yes. I do trust you, Octavia."

"Then show me your face, Modo. I beg of you. So I might know you. It's as simple as removing that mask."

It *was* that simple. He could just lower the mask, show his true self and be done with it. But his hand faltered as he raised it.

His face was not a face. It was a horrid hole where a face should be. She would take one look and that would be the end of everything. He couldn't show her now. Not ever. He was ugly. Mr. Socrates had told him so. He saw it himself every day.

"You cannot look at my real face," he said, surprised that his voice quavered only a little. "No one can ever see it."

She inhaled softly. "Very well," she said, and silently walked into the house and was gone.

Modo got up and went to the railing to stare out at the gardens. This was the way things had to be. It was better for both of them. Yes. It was.

The birds began singing again. The sun was bright in the sky.

Hanging Day

Oscar Featherstone awakened early on the morning of his hanging. Birdsong drifted through the arrow-slit window. The simple, beautiful melody brought tears to his eyes.

His lawyer had been a bone-thin man with the peculiar name of Dubney Swinder and the odd habit of wearing a yellow cravat that made his pale face appear translucent. Oscar, his hope long since gone, had recognized the lacklustre nature of his barrister. The court session had been over in less than ten minutes; the rotund judge in his white wig banged the gavel, and his pronouncement of death by hanging reverberated: "The court doth order you to be taken from hence to the place from whence you came, and thence to the place of execution, and that you be hanged by the neck until you are dead. And may the Lord have mercy upon your soul!"

Oscar's mother, wearing her black crepe dress and waving a black handkerchief, had begun to wail uncontrollably from the gallery as two Beefeaters hauled him back to the prisoner wagon.

The trial was only two days ago. In a few short hours Beefeaters would place him in the same wagon and haul him to the gallows in Newgate Prison. His only consolation was that there would be no crowds. Public hangings had been banned several years ago. The hangman would have to be there, of course.

A key clicked in the cell door but Oscar didn't bother to raise his head. Part of him wanted to grab on to the bars of his cell and hold tight, forcing a scene and making them drag him out of the prison, but another part didn't really care how the next few hours of his life went. The door swung open, rusty hinges screeching. A Beefeater holding a lantern entered. "Oscar Featherstone," he said.

"Yes."

"It is time."

"No. No." Oscar swallowed the lump in his throat. *Maintain your dignity*, he told himself. "It's too early."

"We must go now. They don't appreciate us being late."

Oscar looked up. It was York, the man who had taken to taunting him by singing in a raspy voice, *"The hangman is a tricky knave, he soon my neck will draw."*

York was all business as he roughly unshackled Oscar from the wall and pushed him out of the cell. It had been weeks since Oscar had walked any distance, and he staggered down the hall, his shackles clanking. They'd already rubbed his flesh raw, and every step hurt.

York grabbed Oscar by the shoulder and pushed him down the hallways of the Lieutenant's Lodging. They encountered one maid, who covered her mouth as they passed.

Oscar was shoved through a door into the open air. He had a moment to look at the sky, then he was thrown into the back of a prisoner wagon and the door was slammed shut. Ravens cawed, chiding him from the top of the Bell Tower. He watched through the bars as the wagon rumbled away from the Tower of London.

It was a little past sunrise, but already costermongers and dockworkers were plodding along the sidewalks of the Tower Bridge to their jobs. A few squinted at the wagon as it passed.

He wondered about the moment when he would know death, and brought his hands to his neck. Would it hurt? Would he see his father again in the afterlife? If so, he would ask for forgiveness. He huddled in the corner, trying to keep his sobs silent.

After what felt like an hour, the wagon stopped and York opened the door. "Get out, and be careful not to bang your head," he said, with an unexpected gentleness. He guided Oscar down to the road.

When Oscar looked up he was shocked speechless.

He was standing just inside the gates of his father's estate.

York unlocked the handcuffs and they clattered to the cobblestone drive.

"I . . . I don't understand. What's happening?"

"You were not responsible for your father's death," York said. In the brightening morning light York seemed shorter and a little hunched over. "They'll hang you for the crime anyway. Justice isn't always on the side of the just."

"But why are you releasing me?"

"I'm not who you think I am."

At that moment, Oscar saw that the man wasn't York. He had very similar features, that was all. "Who—who are you?"

He grabbed Oscar's shoulder firmly. "Listen carefully, Mr. Featherstone. You have very little time. March into that house, shave off your beard, cut and colour your hair with shoe polish and disguise yourself in your servant's clothes. Ask your mother for money, as much as possible, and tell her she must never admit you were here. Do not imagine, even for a second, that it would be safe for you to hide out in England. Take the first boat you can find to America or Australia. Do this within the half-hour." He unlocked Oscar's leg manacles. "Go now!"

"Thank you. I thank you," Oscar said, nearly weeping with relief.

"It was the right thing to do," the man said over his shoulder as he walked away. "Mrs. Finchley would be proud of me."

Not quite believing any of the last few minutes could be real, Oscar Featherstone watched the man climb back onto the wagon and ride through the front gate towards the rising sun. Then Oscar ran into his home to find his mother.

ARTHUR SLADE is the author of *Dust*, a national best-seller and winner of a Governor General's Award, the Mr. Christie's Book Award and a Saskatchewan Book Award. *Tribes* was a CLA Young Adult Honour Book and was nominated for five other literary prizes; *Megiddo's Shadow* won a Saskatchewan Book Award and was a Red Maple Honour Book; and *Jolted* was nominated for several Saskatchewan Book Awards. Slade is the author of *Monsterology*, *Villain-ology* and the Canadian Chills series. He lives in Saskatoon. Visit him at **www.arthurslade.com**.

To receive updates on author events and new books by Arthur Slade, sign up at www.authortracker.ca.